The
Spirit
of

David

The
Spirit
of
David

*A Collection
of Inspiring
Stories from
Those Who
Have Overcome...
Winning
Against
All Odds*

*Written and
Compiled by
Ernie Weckbaugh
for
Margaret Schumacher
and her beloved David*

10 9 8 7 6 5 4 3 2 1

ISBN 1-881474-50-X
Library of Congress Catalog Card Number 2003106352

Published by Best-Seller Books and Casa Graphics, Inc.,
Burbank, California • casag@wgn.net
for the Book Publicists of Southern California
www.bookpublicists.org.

Book layout, cover design, and illustrations by Ernie Weckbaugh
of Casa Graphics, Inc., Burbank, California.

Manufactured in the United States of America

David T. Schumacher, Ph.D.

Dedication

To David Theodore Schumacher
whose abilities, love, and generosity
knew no bounds. His example will
remain an inspiration to millions.

Acknowledgments

I am deeply honored by and grateful to Ernie and Patty Weckbaugh of Casa Graphics, President and Vice President of the Book Publicists of Southern Calif., for creating the theme for this unique book. For Patty and Ernie this is a dream come true. Their hard work, enthusiasm and dedication is so much appreciated. It is a privilege to work with you both for such a worthy cause. All proceeds from this book will be donated to charity.

I also wish to thank Irwin Zucker, Founder—Book Publicists of So. Calif., as my PR at Promotion in Motion, Hollywood, for all his suppport of David and I for the last 20 years. An equally big thanks to our editor Lael Littke, best-selling author and professional educator. Without the loyal support of these fine people, this book would not have been possible.

Thank you to Randall Melby, Attorney; Patrick Liddell, Real Estate Attorney, and Moe Saleem Rawda, Tax Accountant and Real Estate Broker for all your guidance and expert advice.

Thank you to David's fine Caregivers who took care of him during the latter years at our home in Hermosa Beach; to Marie Brydl, and to Tavo Rivas for their support, and help with David whenever we took outings and trips. To Eddie Ferrer, caregiver for the last two years of David's life at the Covington, to Scott Garrett, driver for As Directed Limousines, and to Minhquang Phan for his exceptional computer services over the last few years. Your help and kindness brought joy, comfort and richness to his life. Although he could not see any of you, he always recognized you by the sound of your voices.

Thanks to all the Physicians and Caregivers at Mission Hospital, Mission Viejo, California, for their exceptional support and care each time David was admitted. A special thanks to Peter Bastone, CEO Mission Hospital; James Fry, Director of Gifts and Estate Planning; Winnie Johnson, Vice President Mission Hospital Foundation; Colleen Henggeler, Major Gifts Assistant; Peter Czuleger, MD, George Schiffman, MD and Chaplain Howard Young who ministered to David. I'm so grateful for all you have done for both David and I. It has been such a great pleasure to know and work with you all.

Sincere and grateful thanks to my wonderful and spritely 95-year-old father, John Dilkes, and thanks to my family of friends and staff at the Covington where I have resided for almost three years. I feel so blessed to call The Covington my home. Your love, warmth, support and great friendship has sustained me in these difficult months since my dearly beloved David departed this life on July 26, 2006.

May this book be an inspiration to all those with disabilities, as well as to caregivers and family who are coping with loved ones with health problems and difficulties. I feel David is driving and guiding me every day. His spirit gives me the strength and will to continue with my projects and charter new waters on my own.

We enjoyed 29 fantastic years together. More than anything I miss holding your warm, soft hand. My darling David, may your memory live in our hearts forever.

Margaret Schumacher.

The Spirit of David

Moving and inspiring us
To overcome our fear.
They strive to win against all odds
Of things we see and hear.

They rise above anxiety
While climbing every hill,
Beyond the limits most of us
Would deem impossible.

They turn the obvious around
And do the very thing
Requiring courage, confidence
In spite of everything.

Those of us whose health abounds
With strength, agility,
Ponder each achievement
Over "disability."

And every time we read of them,
Realizing they have won,
We once again are so in awe
Of everything they've done.

Ernie Weckbaugh

Preface

Overcoming Adversity
by Danny Quintana, Esq.

"When sorrows come, they come not as single spies—but in battalions."
—Wm. Shakespeare, Hamlet, Act IV, Scene V (Claudius)

I'm an athlete who has been confined to a wheelchair since age 21. My attitude is simple: "I play the cards I have been dealt as they are, not as I hoped they would have been. I spend my time working on the many things I can do and don't waste precious moments thinking about what I cannot do."

The age-old question is: "What motivates some people to overcome adversity and succeed, when so many who have life handed to them often fail?" Part of the world I created for myself is completed in a variety of wheelchair sporting activities, participating fully in my chosen profession, and helping people. As I have traveled around the country competing at various national wheelchair tennis tournaments, I have socialized with brave athletes who've overcome physical disabilities to succeed not just in tennis, but in life. I think of my friend Dean, born with spina bifida, who is a medical scientist with several patients, and an excellent tennis player/instructor.

Then there is Mike, a motivational speaker and former Para-Olympic athlete. He was accidentally shot when he was 16. His attitude is, "If you can't stand up, stand out." Other friends are world-class tennis players. I think about Ester, the world's number one women's wheelchair tennis player. She has not lost a match in over five years, speaks five languages, and is strikingly beautiful. I have played doubles with Anatoly, a charming 60-year-old Russian who was shot down in Afghanistan during the ill-fated invasion during the Soviet era. I taught tennis to the Afghan war wounded at the stadium where the Taliban and Al Qaeda murdered people during their vicious occupation. I've often wondered if one of my students shot down Anatoly's helicopter. Hopefully, these students are still alive. Unfortunately there were no antibiotics for treatment when I was there in November of 2004.

I have met various individuals who, by accident in life or misfortune at birth, have had to compete without limbs. My disabled friends are fierce competitors. Most are wonderful people. The successful ones have a positive attitude about life. Some are computer technicians, bankers, graphic designers, financial analysts, coaches, attorneys, musicians, where so many others are just slugs or underachievers.

When I worked at the Utah State prison I met individuals who, while gifted physically, possessed horrible, debilitating attitudes. The "rules" did not apply to them because they were very strong physically. Others blamed their lot in life on bad parenting or that they were unwanted children striking back at society because "life is not fair." They were right. Life is not fair, it was never fair, and never will be fair. They needed to get used to this rather stark reality.

During my work with the Mobility Project, distributing wheelchairs to the disabled, or in my own world travels I have met wonderful individuals. Many of them struggle with physical and mental problems, in poor countries such as Afghanistan, Costa Rica, Mexico and Thailand. There is Chai, a Thai four-time Gold-Medalist racer in the Para-Olympics. He is a winner in sports and life, because he trains harder and plays smarter than his competitors. Chai understands the price of success and pays it.

However, most people with serious disabilities are not world-class athletes. Yet they work as attorneys, photographers, store clerks, government workers and/or for nonprofit organizations. Some choose not to work and just live out their lives. But thanks to modern medicine and the advances in societal attitudes, millions throughout the world with serious medical problems overcome their adversity and live productive lives.

Then there is the adversity brought on by self-inflicted disabilities due to poor choices. Millions who abuse food and fail to exercise are prone to obesity, diabetes, and hypertension. Millions are brought low by alcoholism and drugs. The solution is to change paths. If we do what we have always done, we will get what we have always got. After all, insanity is doing the same thing over and over again and expecting a different result. Addiction is very difficult to overcome. But it can be done with patience, honesty, and determination. I have seen people lose weight, quit drinking, and stop drug use.

In looking at my own life, I don't speculate on what it would have been like had I not contracted transverse myelities that left me paralyzed when I was a college athlete. There is no point. I cannot change the past and neither can others. My story of overcoming adversity is not any more special or difficult than anyone else.

My biological mother died before I was three, followed four years later by father's remarriage to my wonderful Mormon stepmother. When I was ten, my father was killed by a drunk driver. Ten years later I was suddenly paralyzed by this transverse myelitis after I'd been successful on the college wrestling team.

By the age of 34 I was divorced and almost broke. I had invested my first two million dollars in wine, women, and gambling. After rebuilding my personal fortune, I attracted a series of users and losers. This led to a second divorce. From this I learned it is better to be alone than lonely in a bad relationship. Long ago I accepted that I cannot change being in a wheelchair, or the fact that some people will never accept me because of my disability. Trust me, my life goes on. I stay busy playing tennis, skiing, playing basketball, scuba diving, trying cases in court, investing, cooking great meals, hosting terrific parties, traveling all over the world, telling bad jokes, laughing, enjoying music, and appreciating God's incredible creations. Along the way I raised a wonderful son, two nephews, won numerous major law cases, several national wheelchair tennis tournaments, dated some beautiful women, had wonderful travel experiences, and helped deliver wheelchairs to the poorest of the poor.

I have had a wonderful life because I plan rather than react to events. Overcoming adversity requires appreciating the importance of time. If we live 'til the age of 85, it is a mere 31,025 days! Of these, we will sleep approximately 11,000 days. Thus we have maybe 20,000 left to play out our script in the theater of life. That's not a great amount of time. We are now in the seventh year of this decade and three months into this year as I write this.

How will we spend our very short 20,000 days? Will we enjoy life and look forward to each day? Or will we dread tomorrow, our work, our relationships, our finances, or our poor health?

Hopefully, we will have learned from yesterday, so today will be tolerable and tomorrow will be wonderful. Greet each day with a smile and an attitude that it may be our last day on earth.

It is better to make every minute count— "Seize the day!" We must laugh at our own foibles. As a sophomoric 50 year old, I watch my diet, causing me not to feel like a tired middle-aged man. I continually compete with others much younger than I on the tennis and basketball courts and in the courts of law. Enjoyment comes from being a participant rather than a spectator. Whether we are able bodied or disabled, we have to be willing to pay the price. To win championships, you must be willing to train like a champion and expect to succeed. Bravery in the face of fear has always marked the upward and inward journey of mankind.

Be sure you anticipate and plan your future, not just wait for events to occur. Remember that comparing yourself to others carries a guarantee of personal misery. Notice that people in great physical condition work out, reasonably wealthy people are conservative with money, and people who enjoy peace in their lives surround themselves with calm and sensible people.

A famous hematologist once stated, "Every part of the body depends on one thing, the successful flow of blood." The following chapters are about people who have learned how to successfully cope with adversity. Like the blood referred to, our ability to cope is the one thing that makes everything else possible.

Table of Contents

Introduction
Overcoming Disabilities and Realizing Dreams

Among mankind's highest ambitions is the pursuit of dreams in spite of shortcomings. Perhaps the quest is all the more sweet if the outcome is regarded by others as impossible.

Individual heroes are honored and praised for triumphing over the physical problems of injury, birth defects, disease or accident, loss of loved ones, or an abusive home. This leaves the observer with a heart full of admiration. Poverty and plague, and the more recent challenges of discrimination and dictatorship have left entire populations suffering, facing the need to overcome.

Our heroes are often those who help speed this recovery and healing process, devoting effort to saving others, correcting the wrongs and sufferings of friends and family.

The most visible heroes are those who realize a life-long dream to one day reflect on a goal accomplished. They set the standards and challenge those who follow.

Our collection of heroes are those who fight against barriers, whether these choices are thrust *on* them, or chosen *by* them in reaching a seemingly unattainable dream. The following chapters illuminate the lives of both the disabled and the dreamers who embrace their challenges with courage.

Close-up sleight-of-hand work by a card or coin wizard leaves the audience wondering if what they are seeing is an illusion or indeed magic. In everyday life miraculous events defy explanation. An idea and a persistence of effort may find their way to a crowd or onto the media, giving inspiration to a few or many.

The desire to live a life of adventure and achievement, as promised in our nation's Declaration of Independence, is ingrained in every freeborn citizen. Whether it be our own or that which enables countless others, it matters not. But they who suffer and sacrifice their way to the top will forever attract the admiration of the majority. Why? Because the secret desire of many is to someday do the same.

These chapters are divided between the self-helpers and those who are dedicated to helping others. Often they do both.

-Ernie Weckbaugh

1

A Man of Vision

by Margaret Schumacher

One bright summer day, August 23, 1919, identical twin boys, David and Paul Schumacher, were born in downtown Los Angeles, California. These two beautiful children were perfect in body and soul except for their eyes. They were defective from the genetically inherited disease called progressive myopia. This was to haunt them for the rest of their lives.

David's godmother, Louisa Behn, was one the first children born in 1856 at Johnson's Landing on Catalina Island, 26 miles off the coast of Southern California. Johnson's Landing was where her father, Johann Behn, a German immigrant, and his wife lived and worked on a small cattle ranch and farm.

Louisa moved to the mainland, and at the tender age of 17 married Henry W. Stoll, who was 34. They settled in Los Angeles, had nine children, and became a very prominent family who established the then famous Soda Water Works.

It was David's mother, Minnie, who knew the Stoll family well. They were school friends, so when Minnie gave birth to the twin boys, David and Paul, at the California Lutheran Hospital, Louisa Stoll, then 80, became their godmother. She had a great influence on them in their formative years.

Family had always been an important part of David's life. His father, Max, was

born in Hann, Germany, a small town near Cologne, and met his future wife, Minnie, when she worked at Hamburger's Department Store in Los Angeles, which later became the May Company.

Minnie and Max married in 1907 and moved to Victorville, California, to a ranch by a river. There they built a home, raised horses and invested in real estate.

A few years later, the nearby town of Taft became a boomtown after oil was discovered in the Kettleman Hills. Max saw a golden opportunity in Taft and decided it was time for the family to move. He started a creamery business that immediately flourished. If someone subsequently started a similar business, Max would buy them out, so he soon had a monopoly.

Max was a pioneer in having the first milk truck drive across the ridge route in 1922 to transport milk into the Los Angeles basin. The Schumacher family has the distinction of being members of the Auto Club of Southern California for over 88 years.

The young twins enjoyed riding the truck alongside the driver. They thought it was great fun and truly an adventure. The truck and trailer would stop at Schumacher's relay station in Greenfield, 10 miles from Bakersfield, to collect milk. This was a daily event even in the fog and snow, with a back-up truck always available. It was cheaper to buy milk in Kern County than in Los Angeles. So it was hauled every night, processed in the creamery in Los Angeles, and delivered to the stores.

The creamery also made cheese, ice cream, and skimmed milk. The large walk-in refrigerators were an ideal hiding place for the twins on long, hot summer days. David and Paul learned from their father Max before they were six to be shrewd in all their many future business dealings.

They later struggled in school to read the blackboard. Both wore thick glasses which the other children ridiculed. But in spite of the mockery, they had the consolation of each other's company.

They enjoyed playing together and had doting parents in an always loving, warm family atmosphere. Their parents, Max and Minnie, gave them a solid moral upbringing and encouraged them from their youth to invest in real estate instead of frivolous items. When they wanted a car, their mother suggested they invest their savings in a small house. She told them the house would bring in more than enough return to have the car they were anxious to purchase. How wise Minnie was.

Imagine their struggle to obtain a driver's license, especially so as the years progressed. David attempted to memorize the vision chart in his desperation to drive. All his life David avoided being reliant on other people to assist him, until he lost his sight completely.

Max and Minnie sent them to a special school, but the boys could not join in the usual sporting activities. They were faced with many restrictions, but always remained positive in their outlook on life. They were able to gain sufficient education to proceed to college and, since his father Max owned a dairy and creamery, David went to the University of California at Davis to study agriculture, and later in life he received a Ph.D., with a major in Real Estate in 1978.

David's love of ice cream almost cost the company all the profits. His cousin Marvin would serve in the creamery, and just as David reached out to take the proffered cone, Marvin would let it drop to the floor. This was among the simple boyish tricks they used to play on each other in those days. Being identical twins, David and Paul got a kick out of playing pranks on friends and visitors since it was almost impossible to tell them apart.

Their father Max bought malt shops in Huntington Park and other locations. He purchased the leases of other malt shops and sold them two or three days later, putting in a clause that the new owners had to purchase milk and ice cream from *his* company exclusively. The twins also became involved at an early age with their mother's real estate transactions and rental properties.

The long hot summers were spent on the coast in Hermosa Beach. The family would rent a beach cottage for 3 to 4 months to escape from the scorching desert sun. They would journey all day by car, and often cousins Marvin and Arliene Boettger would join them. It was a time of relaxation, life at a leisurely pace with family get-togethers and outings. These were the days in the late '30s before TV when you made your own entertainment. They listened to the radio or gramophone recordings, went to the movies at the local Bijoux Theatre, or swam in the salt water "plunge."

The red street car went from downtown Los Angeles through Santa Monica, Culver City, and Venice to as far as Redondo Beach. Now there are buildings as far one can see; then on either side of the track there was nothing but row upon row of orange trees. The children would often go on trips to Venice Beach and sail in a boat along the Venice canal waterway. This was long before Venice's streets were put in.

Even though David and Paul had poor eyesight since birth, their parents tried to let them lead as normal a life as possible. Both children grew up in a very loving and positive environment, based on strong religious beliefs and constant encouragement that all things were possible.

The family remained very close, not only in early childhood years but all through both parent's lives. After Minnie passed away in 1945, David and Paul traveled the world extensively with their father. They spent four months in South America and went to Europe countless times. They would visit relatives in various parts of Germany. David couldn't speak to them as he never learned the language, but these were happy times, full of fond memories.

There are peaks and valleys throughout all our lives, and David Schumacher's life was no exception. Difficult times lay ahead. David suffered the loss of his father Max in 1961, followed a decade later by the devastating loss of his twin brother Paul from a migratory brain tumor. Nephew Paul Michael also left the world, at the age of 35, after many months of alcohol abuse. David along with his niece, Dorothy, and sister-in-law, Georgie, were distraught. More stressful times lay ahead for David as he struggled with the ever progressive deterioration of his eyesight.

While cruising on the Nordic Prince in the Caribbean, our lives suddenly turned around when David and I met. With my parents, John and Mabel Dilkes, we soon established a close bond of friendship when they discovered that David and my dad were both real estate appraisers from very different parts of the world. I was 25 years younger, born in Nottingham, Robin Hood's territory in England. Ironically, it was love at first sight since David still saw reasonably well back then. We all spent the remainder of that first cruise together. David and I were married in England in 1977. As soon as it was legally possible, John and Mabel emigrated to America and settled in a beautiful home in Redondo Beach, just three miles from us. David now had a supportive new family. David had always worried about getting married. He was deeply concerned about producing children who, in turn, might lose their sight.

Our first major setback occurred when David suffered a detached retina three months after our wedding. Surgically repaired, the retina detached again later, and he lost the sight of his left eye completely. I stood by him through it all. Here I was in a strange new environment, sustained only by my love for David. I knew that we could weather this storm together.

As a foursome we traveled extensively, with several trips to Hawaii and exotic cruises to Canada, Mexico, the Far East and the South Pacific. The last major event before my dear mother passed away was the grand celebration of her 80th birthday in mid-December, 1994. Our new friend, Tavo Rivas, helped organize this magnificent formal dinner for about 90 relatives and friends. There was a sixty-member choir with violins and trumpets entertaining the guests. This marked the beginning of other large and elaborate parties that followed a few years later. These spectacular events included relatives and friends from all walks of life and from all parts of the globe. Everyone was treated like one of the family.

At my father's 85th birthday party, a Marilyn Monroe lookalike arrived, sat on his knee, and helped everyone sing happy birthday. Then another lookalike, Her Majesty Queen Elizabeth, arrived, complete with regalia and crown along with a Tower of London Beefeater. She came to bestow the honor of knighthood on John, to the delight of the guests.

Five years later, David's 80th birthday party was aboard the Fantasy One luxury yacht in Marina del Rey that featured a singer/songwriter and a famous magician from the Magic Castle in Hollywood. The highlight of the evening was when a stunning mermaid made a surprise appearance on the yacht.

Recently on the Internet there was a statement with which we all agree. It described the word "family" as Father And Mother, I Love You. Throughout our married life, my father John, David and I remained a close family who enjoyed warmth, friendship, and a deep love.

At 40 years of age, David had lost all of his money in the commodities market. It was a devastating blow. He figured he knew more about the real estate field and became a very successful appraiser. Paul did likewise. They both worked hard and played hard. David appraised the Los Angeles "Follies" (the costume collection, not the glamorous show girls inside the fancy garments). He appraised properties on Catalina Island, spending three months there, and appraised many of the casinos and hotels in Las Vegas.

Paul passed away at the early age of 51. David struggled through the grief and carefully planned the course of his life knowing full well he might be totally blind one day. In his spare time, David traveled extensively around the world as both a tourist and a tour leader. He reveled in unusual situations as his way of getting thrills. He delighted in having a huge snake draped around his neck in Bangkok.

In Lagos, Nigeria, a peddler threw a big black spider onto David's head when he refused to purchase a second carved statue. Everyone screamed as the spider crawled down David's neck. He hastily knocked the creature to the ground, but the incident could have had deadly consequences. In Papua, New Guinea, he bravely put his hand in the water to feel baby crocodiles swimming beside his canoe on the Sepik River.

His continuing eye problems could not deter our desire for travel and adventure. David and I were among the first American tourist groups to journey to China and Mongolia in 1979. We survived a monstrous hurricane on the Fiji Islands. Near the Ross River, outside Alice Springs, Australia, we spend the night in a bus that listed at a 45-degree angle in mud surrounded by torrents of swirling water.

Throughout our married life, David and I have spent less than six months apart. We communicated well and learned to exchange our life's roles. First David was the decision maker, then, when his sight diminished, I took over as the dominant role. In this marriage of great learning, David taught me many vital lessons regarding the real estate business with its multiple facets, and how to promote his book on real estate, *Buy and Hold, 7 Steps to a Real Estate Fortune.*

We learned to adapt to living with blindness. Suddenly everything at home had to be in its proper place all the time to avoid accidents.

Trips away from home had to involve accommodations for the disabled for safety and comfort. People with a severe disability want to be treated like otherwise normal people, and David would like people not to know, but it's difficult trying to lead a normal life when you're unable to see.

His greatest contribution was to write a book after he lost his sight so he could share his real estate knowledge and the method by which he acquired his wealth. Not a day passed that he was not an inspiration to our friends and to me.

He reveled in helping people with their real estate problems, receiving numerous phone calls on a daily basis. David yearned to give back a few of the great rewards he had received while he was still of strong mind and body. He was able to make an outstanding recovery from a stroke.

He was full of boundless energy. During his appraisal years, David would tackle five projects at the same time. He was a humble man with tremendous persistence and determination. If something did not go right the first or second time he would try again.

David was a walking encyclopedia. Before he lost his eyesight he had memorized all the streets in downtown Los Angeles, and by someone describing the buildings he knew exactly where he was. He was a shining star in the world of darkness. A winner in the game of life. He never gave up. He found something good to say about everyone he met. He was always positive. The word negative did not exist in David's vocabulary.

In the last months of his life he was hospitalized four times at Mission Hospital, in Mission Viejo, California, where he received the excellent compassionate care he richly deserved. David enjoyed the wonderful harpist who played throughout the hospital during the weekends. The calming music surely aided in the healing of the patients. The caregivers and physicians were exceptional. This was vital for someone who could not see. He depended on others 24/7. Touch became more and more important in his final weeks and days as he struggled with congestive heart failure, pulmonary edema and a severe aortic stenosis.

It was the only period in his life, never wanting to be alone for even a single moment, when he became extremely anxious. Although weakened by illness, David, his mind ever-learning and searching, sensed that Mission was a fine, progressive hospital with exciting goals for expansion for the future. When completed, The Schumacher Healing Garden at Mission Hospital (rendering on the facing page) will be a fitting memorial to David's undying spirit, and it will be a place where others may find healing of Body, Mind and Spirit. Just like David, always thinking of doing for others.

He was impressed to learn that Mission Hospital is one of the nation's

Schumacher Healing Garden

top ten hospitals for the treatment of heart attacks and bypass surgery, and that it was the only community hospital in Orange County certified as a stroke receiving hospital.

The emergency room has just doubled in size and David truly felt that his life was extended by several months from all the exceptional care and attention he received. By divine providence, David spent his final days on earth in Mission Hospital where his spirit transitioned into Eternity with dignity and peace.

His life had been the story of a man of many dreams and goals, most of which he'd *made* happen through persistence and a great zest for life.

2

Claire's First Song

by Barbara Varma

"**S**he's what?" the professor asked in surprise as if he were the one who couldn't hear. "She's deaf," I said again, quickly adding, "and I'm her interpreter."

The professor's stare remained on me despite my explanation. I couldn't fault his reaction. After all, we were standing in his Beginning Piano class.

My client, Claire, in her late 20s, fidgeted from behind her front-row keyboard. The professor glanced her way as if he doubted her inability to overhear his concern.

"But," he said with intention, "this is a piano class. If she can't hear, how can she learn to play?"

How, indeed? Truth was, I'd been wondering the same thing myself but my interpreter training compelled me to keep such thoughts quiet. I turned to face Claire.

"YOU DEAF," I signed. "CAN'T HEAR PIANO. HOW YOU LEARN?"

Understanding now, Claire smiled at her teacher and signed: "ME REGISTER FOR CLASS."

"I've registered for this class," I said, voicing for her.

"THAT MY INTERPRETER."

"That's my interpreter."

"SHE INTERPRET FOR ME."

"She'll translate everything for me."

The professor's head turned from to side to side, unsure of which one of us to look at.

Claire dropped her hands, calmly waiting for him to respond. If she understood the inherent complexity of having a deaf student in a music class, she gave no clue, continuing to regard her new instructor with steady expectation. He quickly turned and retreated to the front of the class, apparently deciding to pursue this puzzle at another time.

I gave Claire a quick, reassuring smile before taking my seat up front, facing her and to the left of the instructor. The professor stood quietly behind his podium; I could still feel the heat of his attention but he didn't challenge my being in "his space."

"This is Beginning Piano," he said and then launched into what seemed to be a well-used speech. As I signed for Claire, the professor sent a few nervous glances our way but for the most part ignored our distraction.

Behind her keyboard, Claire sat perfectly still. She looked young for a woman with two children, her youthful appearance accentuated by round wire-rimmed glasses. It was easy to see she was excited about the class; hazel eyes drank in every sign, every expression, eager to take in the professor's words. When he instructed the students to "Play a C chord," Claire placed her hands gingerly on the keys.

"Begin," said the professor with a downward wave of his baton.

"BEGIN," I signed.

A variety of sounds filled the room, some of which I

recognized as a C chord, others not. Claire's was in the latter category, but being unable to hear her mistake, she continued to hold the discordant chord with confidence. The professor heard the sour chime and looked around for its source, tilting his head to guide him in. He approached Claire and bent down to correctly position her hands, then strode back to the front of the class but not before directing a telling gaze my way: *This isn't going to work.*

He raised his baton to cue a second attempt. Challenged now, I quickly gained Claire's attention and signed "AGAIN," my right hand moving up and over in a half-circle arc to land in the waiting palm of my left. Luckily, she got it right this time and won the chance to continue.

Her first exam didn't go well, causing the professor to look slightly smug behind his normal reserve. As an interpreter, I've been conditioned to be the anonymous third party, present to communicate, not intervene. But as I heard the discordant chords crying from Claire's keyboard, I realized I had to do more.

I obtained permission to also tutor Claire and made an unscheduled appearance at her next practice session. She was pleased but puzzled to see me. I explained that since I also knew how to play the piano, I was assigned to coach as well as interpret her lessons, but first I needed to know something.

"CLAIRE," I signed, "WHY YOU WANT LEARN PLAY-PIANO?"

"MY FAMILY LOVE MUSIC," she replied and described the various instruments she'd seen her hearing family play. Her husband played the guitar, her sister the flute and her young daughter the violin. Then her eyes shone even more brightly as she paraded her fingers up and down an imaginary keyboard, swaying her body side to side for added effect.

"Who plays the piano?" I signed, eyebrows raised to form the question.

"No one, but I've seen others play and I think it's very pretty." Her hands moved quickly, confidently.

I still wasn't convinced. "But Claire, how will you do it? I mean, you can't hear the notes…"

Claire became very serious, her chin rising in a stubborn pose. "I just want to play one song, a Christmas song, that's all. I know I can do it and then I'll play it for my family at Christmas. It will be pretty," her hands insisted.

"Okay," I agreed. "We can learn a song. I know how to play the piano and could help you practice if you like." Claire smiled and nodded, the universal sign for YES.

She chose a Christmas carol, ironically *Silent Night,* to be her one and only performance for both family and professor. We practiced it often until I heard the famous tune continually—though she, of course, was spared the mental reruns.

The final exam landed on a chill winter's day. Claire arrived on time, her hair slightly mussed from the wind. The professor gestured toward the piano with a slight bow, intent on extending the dignity of the situation despite his misgivings. Looking at me he asked, "What song shall she play?"

I knew the answer, of course, but relayed the question to Claire.

"SILENT NIGHT," she replied, her hands making a graceful path in the air. The professor's hands rose and for a moment I thought he was going to try the signs on, but his hands remained quiet by his side.

"Fine," he said and nodded. She began, and the familiar tune of *Silent Night* filled the room.

I wish she could have heard it. It was perfect. Each note a confirmation of her desire to do something they said she couldn't do. My mind filled in the missing lyrics just as her hands filled in the silence. *"Silent night, Holy night. All is calm, all is bright..."*

Finally the last ringing tone faded away, the effect guided by a slow release of her hands from the ivory keys.

"Why...that's incredible!" the professor said, staring at her in amazement. "I wouldn't have believed it..." He turned towards me. "I wonder...could she play it for me again?"

He studied my hands as they signed "AGAIN" and then turned back to Claire. Awkwardly his right hand moved up and over in a small half-circle arc to land in the middle of his left palm. "AGAIN." The professor's first sign.

She smiled, and began the song again.

As *Silent Night* once again filled the room I surveyed the scene: Claire, the piano, and the professor. Claire was right, I decided.

It really was very pretty.

3

For the Love of Dancing

by Lori Hartwell

The teenage years are the time for acquiring an education, learning independence, and gaining social skills. Most teens also attend their schools' proms and cherish the memories.

However, not everyone has that opportunity. A teenager with kidney disease misses much of the usual school experience because of prolonged absences. I never had the opportunity to attend my own prom, because I was recovering from a failed second transplant. We who are afflicted become too familiar with life and death issues. Because of this, we often cannot communicate with our "well" teen counterparts. In my teen years, I was dealing with serious issues and my peers were dealing with how to get a date, so we never really connected. This situation can leave you feeling isolated.

Having lived with complete kidney failure since the age of 12 and spending the next 12 years on dialysis, I understand teenagers with kidney problems. The reality of kidney disease is that you can live a long and healthy life, but one of the key ingredients for living a successful life is connecting with others who understand your particular brand of experience. "One friend can make the difference."

With this in idea in mind, I decided to organize a prom for teenagers with kidney disease. My non-profit group, the Renal Support Network (RSN), and its dedicated volunteers helped create an evening the teens will cherish for a lifetime.

Not knowing what type of evening today's teenagers would enjoy, we consulted with experts: teenagers. Several students from

Notre Dame High School in Sherman Oaks, California, volunteered their time and "cool" perspective on how to make the evening one they would always remember. On January 20th, 2002, we held our third annual prom, "For the Love of Dancing." Each year the kidney teen attendance grows, showing a need for events geared toward teens. This year we topped 150 guests. Every year the Notre Dame Senior Class is very curious about kidney disease and eager to help. They donate their entire weekend to decorating the school cafeteria into a classy nightclub environment. They then change their clothes and act as hosts for the evening. If they see someone who is not dancing, they encourage them to join in the fun. This is the distinct difference between a normal prom and ours. Nobody is rejected.

The volunteer teens are amazing, and they become very interested in the teens they host for the evening. The RSN presents an educational program on kidney disease and some of the obstacles that these special teens will have to overcome. One of the Notre Dame teens cautiously asked the question, "Are these kids going to die?" Once we explained how kidney disease is treated, they became more optimistic and not so afraid of the unknown. The students asked a lot of great questions, which helped tremendously with the volunteer teens relating to the kidney teens.

They showed so much enthusiasm for making the prom into a success, it was contagious. The inspiration spread to many people who offered to volunteer time and donate prom dresses. The RSN received a collection of prom dresses, some even mailed anonymously. Mary Mentser, a nephrology nurse at Children's Hospital, assisted many eager young prom attendees to choose a dress hanging on a rack in her office. Many young girls who are on dialysis come from low-income families and cannot afford to purchase a new dress for the prom. The dresses are hemmed and fitted for each of the girls who would otherwise go without one.

The Big Night of the event is always held on the Sunday of Martin Luther King Weekend. This way we do not have to worry about dialysis schedules, and the teens do not have to go to school the next day. At 5 p.m., they began to arrive in cars and vans, and suddenly the entire parking lot area filled up with teenagers.

In a room adjacent to the dance area, Leslie Holden, RN organized volunteers that help the girls with their make-up and hair in preparation for a glamour photo. When I peeked into the room, I watched them wrapping feather boas around their necks and trying on different costume jewelry. So much fun!

One of the teenage boys said, "I didn't know girls on dialysis could be so pretty!" New romance was in the air. Laura, a transplant patient for 14 years now, heard about the prom from a staff worker at Children's Hospital in Los Angeles. This was her first year in attendance, and she couldn't have had a better time. When asked what her favorite part of the prom was, Laura replied with a wide smile, "The dancing!" She was one of the first guests to hit the dance floor and she rarely missed a song. She took a short break when "Madonna" arrived to awe the teens with her lip-syncing abilities, but that break was short lived. Laura was the first person chosen to take center stage with the impersonator and danced center stage once again when "Jennifer Lopez" arrived. Laura wasn't the only one having a good time. Matthew, a dialysis patient, didn't allow his wheelchair to hold him back from having fun. He was one of several kidney patients who took advantage of the 15-minute limo rides that cruised down Ventura Boulevard. When he returned, he glided onto the dance floor and moved back and forth to the sounds of disco. His evening was topped off when he heard his name called as the winner of a mystery prize — something he had been talking about all evening.

Robin Siegal, Licensed Clinical Social Worker, says that the Renal Prom allows the teens to come out of their shell. "Patients often feel like there is a stigma that comes with kidney disease," Siegal said. "This event allows them to let their guard down."

The teens are free to communicate and be carefree—there are even translators available for the teens who speak Spanish only. The prom also provides hope for young adults living with kidney disease. Malia Langen is a transplant recipient who attended last year's prom, and this year she offered to volunteer. "Growing up, I was always the youngest patient in the dialysis unit, so I felt like I was the only teenager who had kidney disease," Langen said. "This prom allows teenagers to meet other young people who are dealing with the same challenges that they are."

Jason Easley agrees, "The first prom I was still on dialysis. The second one I received my transplant. It's a wonderful night because it allows us to meet so many other kids. Sometimes we forget we're not the only ones having this problem, and a night like this lets us see and meet other teens like us outside of a hospital room." An event program booklet was provided that included blank pages, soon filled with an exchange of phone numbers and email addresses. The interaction with the kidney teens also benefited many of the Notre Dame students who admitted that they had some misconceptions about kidney teens. However, those assumptions were nullified on prom night when they found themselves laughing and dancing among the guests. Student volunteer Amanda Fuller says that it has been a learning experience she'll never forget. "I learned that these kids look and act just like I do," Fuller said. "At first I thought that I would have nothing in common with them, but now I realize that I do and that there is no reason to assume that we are different." This sentiment is an added bonus to the wonderful effect that the prom has on the community. It is an event where everyone wins.

Long time volunteer and nurse administrator, Sue Vogel, says that the prom allows renal care professionals to see their patients in a different light. "Most of the kidney patients I care for are elderly," Vogel says. "It is refreshing to see these young kidney patients who are so vibrant and full of life! It reminds me of how important encouragement and hope is to them, and it motivates me to help provide that as a renal care professional."

Many renal care professionals understand that they can have an impact in and outside of the hospital. Offering their time at the prom is just one way they are able to show the teens that they care. Their presence at the prom also provides parents who chauffeur their teens the opportunity to ask questions in a different environment. Parents and renal care professionals often take advantage of the opportunity to mingle in a separate room made available for volunteers.

Another room is also set-aside specifically for teens to do a dialysis exchange—if necessary—and a dialysis nurse volunteers her time to be there to assist them with any questions. We have never had a request to do a PD exchange, but the room serves to increase renal awareness. It's a subtle reminder of what it's like to live with kidney disease. Just like the bottles of Tums that are put on the buffet table, the teens may or may not need them on prom night, but their presence usually persuades the volunteers to ask why they are being made available. This prom acts as a conversation piece—one with so many elements put forth to trigger curiosity and to educate. For example, many of the Notre Dame teens asked about organ donation issues and what can they do to help their teen peers. There are so many people who benefit from the prom every year in so many different ways, especially the teens. The biggest obstacle is getting them there. Coordinating transportation proves one of the biggest tasks, and last-minute changes are always imminent. Each year there are more than eighty teens needing transportation. This year we contacted all of the volunteers and even solicited new ones to ask if they would be responsible for picking up a teen and guest and taking them home after the event. Dr. Gary Lerner and his wife agreed to be chauffeurs, escorting one of his patients and her guest.

One volunteer picked up five kids and drove them over 120 miles to the event. I was told later that everyone was a little quiet on the way up, but the ride home was full of non-stop laughter and recapping of the night's events, as well as asking the driver if they could stop at a coffee shop.

Renal disease is too demanding if you do not have hope. I'd accomplished one of my personal missions. Helping teens connect with someone who understands.

Most importantly, the teens had the opportunity to make friendships and ask questions, like: what to expect when they get called for a transplant; how do they live a joyful life in spite of renal disease? and the most important question; "When do you tell a potential date you have kidney failure?"

In addition, it's never too late to fulfill one of your dreams. Now 37, I often regretted not having the chance to attend my own prom, but now I get to attend one each year with my wonderful husband, Dean.

4

That Awful Mountain

by Dr. Hal Browder

It seemed as though I had seen this view of the Matterhorn in Switzerland before, since I had for years been fascinated by its history and read many books on its mystique. Here I was at last in the town of Zermatt looking at that "Awful Mountain," as it was so described by those early mountaineers who first viewed its summit. The Matterhorn, at 14,691 feet, is not the tallest mountain, even in the Alps. But since it stands out as an isolated citadel, it represents an awesome, intimidating sight.

Early climbers had looked at the Hornli Ridge facing the town and deemed it too steep to attempt, so they turned their attention to the Italian side of the mountain. These early mountaineers came close to reaching the summit from the Italian side, but were for various reasons unable to reach their goal. It was British mountaineer, Edward Whymper, who decided that the ridge facing Zermatt would, as climbers state, "GO!"

Well, here I was in Zermatt gazing at this sight. All the effects of jet lag seemed to drain away as I looked on this mountain and wondered if I could indeed climb to its top pinnacle. To start my quest of the peak, I had to first go to the Bergfuhrer's office to see about teaming up with a Swiss mountain guide to join me in a climb of the peak.

I was told there had been a rather late and heavy snowfall in that area this year and that the peak was deemed too iced up to safely climb in its present condition. What a disappointment it was since I had only a few days before I had to return to Los Angeles and back to my dental practice. The guide service offered as an alternative a climb of the Rimpfischhorn, which is a worthy peak, but certainly not the Matterhorn. I grudgingly signed up to do this climb in a few days.

Because I had been rather inactive for a few weeks, I spent the next two days doing some hiking around Zermatt to gain some conditioning before doing a major climb. One day was spent hiking and climbing the Mettelhorn, which is a peak of 11,900 feet that rises high above the west wall of Zermatt Valley. The view from the top of this peak was fantastic, especially the precipitous east face of the Wiesshorn and the north face of the Matterhorn. I was joined on top of the peak by a German couple, and we took in the view and shared some delicious chocolate treats.

The next day I checked in at the Bergfuhrer's office to confirm my climb of the Rimpfischorn. Well, much to my elation and surprise, I was told that the Matterhorn would be guided the next day by the classic Hornli Ridge route. I was lucky that there was a guide available to do the climb. It was there I met my guide, Lucky Imbroden, who informed me that we needed an early start. He said we needed to be on our way no later than 3:30 a.m. Up in my room I met my roommates, one Canadian and two Polish climbers who were playing cards and chain smoking.

Sleep did not come easy, and the view out the window looked straight up the frightening ridge I was soon to be climbing. I felt that I had just dozed off when a hand touched my back with a voice saying, "Up mountain man; we have a peak to climb."

I jumped up and grabbed my gear and went down to the usual European breakfast made up of hard rolls and very strong coffee. Equipment for the day consisted of crampons, wind parka, wool knickers, gaiters, wool shirt, a pair of leather gloves, wool mittens and a wool balaclava for head protection.

Lucky and I roped up just outside the hut and fitted headlamps for light, and off we went into the darkness. We hit our departure time right at 3:30 a.m., and we were luckily near the front of the five or six parties doing the climb this day. Very soon we hit the first steep rocks marking the ridge, and my guide cautioned me about the icy conditions we would encounter. It would not take much to misstep, especially in the early morning darkness. No sooner than warned of this hazard, I heard a scraping, sliding sound ahead. With a taut rope in hand, my embarrassed Swiss guide was about ten feet below me. It was needless to say, at that juncture, I wondered if I had made a good choice and if I really wanted to be on this mountain at all!

Lucky scrambled back on route and, in silence, off we went again. We climbed on in silence, with Lucky's only utterances being, "Up, up, mountain man!" Finally, at a short rest break, I turned to him and said, "Don't worry about the slip; we're doing great, so let's have a good time." That broke the tension, and for the rest of the climb, he was very talkative and he pointed out all the historical spots where various events took place on this "class" climb.

Looking back it was quite a sight with the headlamps of the following climbers looking like a chain of one-eyed monsters in pursuit. Soon, first light was breaking in the west, and what an amazing scene it was with the surrounding peaks being illuminated with a fiery red glow.

The air was crisp and the rock was solid as we moved together up the ridge to reach the Solvay Hut perched precariously on a rocky outcropping.This shelter was erected for house climbers who were caught on the ridge in bad weather or who were injured and awaiting rescue.

Above the hut, the angle of the ridge increased on meeting Moseley Slabs, named for an American climber who fell to his death while attempting the climb. We were now climbing in mixed bare rock and iced sections of the ridge, and we had fastened crampons to our climbing boots. Crampons, whose metal spikes clattered and gave off sparks on hitting the rocks, made the climbing seem awkward indeed. Nevertheless, up we climbed.

At the Swiss Shoulder, the angle eases off, but soon you reach the terrifying north-facing snow and ice covered section whose angle reaches to 40 degrees. Here you are very aware of the exposure, since you are now looking straight down the 4,000-foot vertical drop of the north face of the mountain.

This section of the climb is protected by some fixed ropes, which aid in climbing this last obstacle before the final summit ridge. Above, I could see no more mountain looming, and soon we were on the summit. Lucky patted me on the back and congratulated me on the climb. Soon, the corniced summit ridge was crowded with other climbers, and we were all braced against the cold, biting wind sweeping the summit. Lucky broke out a flask, and we toasted with some highly sugared warm drink. The view was wonderful!

You look down the Italian side of the mountain to the small villages below. In the distance you could make out Mount Blanc, the Monte Rosa and even the Jungfrau area of Switzerland. The ascent had taken three hours and twenty minutes, with one formal stop to put on crampons.

We spent about thirty minutes on top taking the usual summit photographs, and talking to some of the other climbers who shared the summit with us. Soon it was time to leave. I have always found the descent of steep mountains more difficult in some ways than the climb up. Going down, you're always facing the exposure, and foot placement seems more difficult. Descending from the summit, you are immediately faced with the view down the vertical north face of the mountain. It was from this point that you encounter the place where disaster struck the first ascending party in 1895, led by Whymper. Four of the seven first ascenders fell down this face to their deaths. Most accidents seem to happen when descending a mountain.

Our careful descent was tedious and time consuming, but we were back to the Hornli Hut by noon. It was good to be off the mountain as early as possible to avoid the rock falls that occur regularly down the mountain as the sun thaws the snow and ice above, releasing any embedded rocks. As it was, we saw and heard a number of significant rock falls down the east-facing chutes as we climbed down.

As tradition dictates, I signed Lucky's guidebook, which is reviewed by the Swiss Mountain Guides Association after each trip. In this book you are asked to comment on how you rated your guide's performance. I rated Lucky Imboden as an excellent guide, which he was. The Imboden family has a long history of mountain guides spanning many generations.

My return to Zermatt and the green surroundings ended a long and exciting day. Once again the mountain's Gods were kind to me, and this was a realization of a long-dreamed fantasy. It was great to hug my family back at the chalet and be thankful for my safe passage.

When looking back on this climb, it reminds me of what one mountain sage once said: "Whom have we conquered?"

"None but ourselves!"

5

She Changed My Life

by Carolyn Brent

W hen I look back to recall which were the special individuals who most influenced my attitudes of what kind of person I could be, and who I wanted to be, one stands out among the others. Her name was Eleanor Roosevelt.

Franklin Delano Roosevelt, as a disabled president, turned to her as a valued partner in influencing the American people. As a syndicated newspaper columnist ("My Day"), and later as the ambassador to the United Nations, she was certainly one of the most admired women in the country. She represented women at a time when women's rights were very limited during the great Depression. It is fair to say at the time that most women were seriously disadvantaged.

In a nutshell, when I got married at the age of nineteen, my mother was neurotic and my mother-in-law was psychotic. I didn't understand then, but simply assumed that was the way all older women were. I thought when I aged I would be like them. It was a frequent way of life for older women.

Then one day when I was attending UCLA, the *Daily Bruin* announced that Eleanor Roosevelt was scheduled to speak in Royce Hall at noon. My morning class was over at eleven, and the afternoon class started at one. Fine. I would eat my lunch after eleven, and then go to the auditorium and hear Mrs. Roosevelt. Talk about naiveté! I showed up at 11:30 a.m. to an overcrowded auditorium, crammed full of a shrieking mass of students screaming and trying to find empty seats for themselves and yelling to their friends.

I walked in the back door and down the left aisle amid the din. The rows of seats were jammed full. I walked down the aisle thinking there might be a single seat somewhere. I got to the fourth row to find the front rows were empty but cordoned off for the press—so I kept walking. Then I realized the very front row was not roped off, and every seat there was also empty.

I boldly walked to the middle of the left side of the aisle and sat down. After a few minutes other people found their way down and that row quickly filled up. I realized we were sitting less than fifteen feet from the apron of the stage, with an unobstructed view of the platform.

Then the curtains opened a little bit, and someone brought out a podium positioning it in the center, close to the front. Then someone else brought out four chairs and placed them in front of the closed curtains, directly in front of us. Then, without any to do, Mrs. Roosevelt and three men came out and occupied those four seats. They were less than twenty feet from me. Mrs. Roosevelt pulled out her knitting and started to work on it.

To cheering and clapping, a university official got everyone's attention and introduced the other officials, who each said a few words. Then, with a short comment, he introduced Mrs. Roosevelt. She put her knitting in her bag and stood at the podium to speak.

She was not beautiful by Hollywood standards. Her voice was high and squeaky. But she possessed a "presence." She exuded dignity. She commanded attention and respect. She talked for more than half an hour, and everything she said was significant, to the point, and riveting. At this time, so many years later, I have no recollection of her message.

What came over me and changed my life was the realization that older women can mature, be significant, speak with clarity and sense and wisdom. It was not written that I had to become neurotic or psychotic. I could continue with learning, developing and changing with the times.

As I write this, I am older than Mrs. Roosevelt was that day; however, after that turning point, I have consciously continued to develop those qualities. Today I can quiet an auditorium full of screaming adolescents. I can speak of things that are significant to them with clarity and wisdom, and they listen to me.

I feel self-confident and affective. Bless you, Eleanor Roosevelt. I will be forever grateful.

6

Back in the Saddle

by Mary Jo Beckman

In the spring of 2006, the Army allowed me to initiate a therapeutic riding program using the Ft. Myer Caisson horses that perform the military funerals in Arlington Cemetery. The riders are wounded servicemen/women who have had amputations or extreme damage to limbs and are in rehabilitation at Walter Reed Army Medical Center. The program had received much publicity since it started in May, with exposure on *CNN, Good Morning America, Pentagon News Channel*, plus numerous magazines and newspapers.

The Secretary of Veterans Affairs visited in early December of 2006 and expressed the desire to expand the program for all wounded warriors.

Decade after decade, the elegant final journey through winding roads of the nation's cemetery has been the last service the horses and the riders of the 3rd United States Infantry give to their comrades in arms.

Now a new service has begun for the storied Caisson Platoon of the Army's "Old Guard," formally known as the 3rd Infantry Battalion, 3rd Infantry Regiment: helping wounded veterans from Iraq and Afghanistan re-learn balance, coordination and other valuable physical therapy skills.

This has been a pilot therapeutic riding program for wounded veterans recuperating at the Walter Reed Army Medical Center in Washington, D.C. Five soldiers and one airman signed up to participate in the first session. It also included a former rodeo trick rider who lost his right leg below the knee to an IED roadside bomb.

Another participant, according to our Caisson Platoon Leader Chief Warrant Officer 4 Abdullah Johnson, was a female enlisted soldier who was depressed over the loss of her lower leg. After she took the first session at Ft. Myer, where the horses are stabled, her mother said, "That's the first time since she got back from Iraq that I've seen a smile on her face."

The medical term for using horses for treatment is hippotherapy, according to Lance Pence, a retired Army command sergeant major who joined me in founding the pilot program. I have been an instructor from the North American Riding for the Handicapped Association.

Around the country, many hippotherapy programs are designed to help children with degenerative diseases such as multiple sclerosis. But horseback riding has also provided a huge benefit for amputees, including the many wounded veterans at Walter Reed.

Adjusting to the motion of the horse helps with core strengthening of the lower back and hips, while taking the pressure and pain off the amputated limbs.

Joseph Backus, who is an occupational therapist at Walter Reed, said he has seen the riders "find a whole new center of balance and a new sense of control during the program."

Army 1st Lieutenant Ryan Kules, who took three of the four lessons that were offered, said, "It has improved my balance each time.

"Also, I'm always looking for things I've done before that I can still do, even after losing an arm and a leg," he continued. "It's a real confidence builder."

7

A Fever to Achieve

by Linnaea Mallette

I was four years old and very, very sick. I remember my mother saying to my older brother, "Your sister has a fever of 106 degrees." I do not recall anything more after that. I do know, however, that I was not taken to a hospital. It could have been because it was 1957 and we lived on a ranch in San Fernando, far from any medical facilities. It could have been that my mom had been drinking and not sensitive to the critical nature of my condition. Or, she may not have been aware that high fevers can damage hearing— and a large part of mine was seared away that night.

Today, even with the assistance of two hearing aids, I am unable to perceive notes at the high end of a piano keyboard. I do not hear birds sing. I've never heard a cricket chirp. I know it is raining by the sound of the rainwater running through the gutter. "Two" and "three" sound nearly the same to me. A person's tone, pitch, rate of speech, visual cues and topic of conversation all work together to carve understanding into the chunks of speech I perceive. Despite much speech therapy, I can't quite wrap my mouth around certain sounds such as "r" or "ch,"— sounds I can't hear, and can only do my best to approximate.

As a child and throughout my school years, I was teased all the time because of my speech impediment. It was awful. So bad, in fact, that I finally dropped out of high school. Mom, as an alcoholic, and dad, who was clinically depressed, gave me the best they could, but it wasn't enough to shore up my crippled self-esteem. How could they? They hardly had any themselves! I learned, after they had both passed (they died within eight months of each other in 1996 and '97), that early in their marriage Mom had tried to talk Dad into the two of them committing suicide together. While they were not great role models, my brother and I never doubted that they loved us with all their hearts. They did the best they could.

In an attempt to find solace from the pervasive feeling of rejection and imperfection, I turned to drugs and alcohol at age 21 and continued to use them to medicate myself well into my 30s. I lived at home until I was 38.

It has been said that the psychology of the handicapped is to work twice as hard to overcome the burden of imperfection. As I look back on my life and how I've always pushed myself, that might be true. Even though drugs and alcohol slowed me down, I didn't wait for life to give me a kick in the pants to grow. I always strived to be the best I could be. As a life-long friend commented during my 50th birthday celebration, "What I've learned from Linnaea is to put one foot in front of the other and keep moving."

Today, it never ceases to amaze me when I notice individuals are nervous while talking to me. ME! The person who, at age 34, locked herself in the bathroom three times and cried because she didn't have enough confidence to talk to the successful people milling around at a party. Me, the person who went for two to three years at a time without any boyfriends or dates. Those who know me and those who learn about me often ask how I've moved from such a state of fear to the confidence I exude today.

I used many tools. One of the most powerful is what I call WOWs – Words Of Wisdom. WOWs are the nourishment for my soul and stimulation for my mind. I live on a steady diet of WOWs, and I encourage others to do the same. Here are some of my most powerful WOWs: "If you can imagine it,
You can achieve it.
If you can dream it,
You can become it."   — *William Arthur Ward*

Adversity did not stop me from envisioning and eventually becoming the person I wanted to be and living the life I wanted to live. I spent countless hours, beginning in junior high school, envisioning myself as popular, an important part of a group—maybe even the center of attention—a leader and able to make a difference in the lives of others.

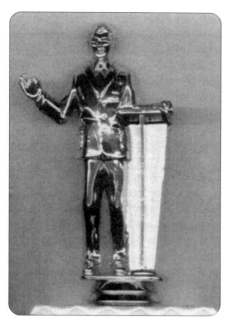

Today I enjoy the company of more friends than I can keep track of. Thanks to a childhood friend who became a cosmetologist, he was able to maximize my appearance, and with his help, even today at age 50, I often enjoy the attention of men nearly half my age.

Thanks to Toastmasters, a nonprofit organization that helps people overcome the common fear of public speaking, my vision of becoming an effective communicator and leader has been fulfilled. I have served as a District Governor, which is the equivalent of running a non-profit organization of nearly 1,500 people with a team of 23 leaders. Through my Toastmaster experience, I am in the position to make meaningful contributions to my community—and I have.

Several years ago, I started a Toastmasters club for recovering alcoholics and drug addicts at a Salvation Army Adult Rehabilitation Center. In 2000, I created a Toastmaster club for the Mary Magdalene Project, a Los Angeles nonprofit group that helps former prostitutes build new lives. I have had several opportunities to orchestrate an Americana Program to honor our vets at a local Disabled American Veterans facility.

Thanks to my vision of being well-schooled in classical music, I was drawn to serve as a volunteer for a local orchestra and introduced myself to the classical violinist who became my husband. I often come home to a quartet practicing in my own living room.

Ah, I could go on for a month of Sundays on the power of envisioning. I encourage people to examine the lives they are living today, for they have most likely visualized it a couple of years ago. "Mind your mind!" I remind my friends. "Find a need and fill it."

—Dr. Earl Barnum

Following the wisdom of this quote has led me to the fulfilling job I enjoy today. I am a training coordinator at UCLA, helping research administrators campuswide understand the myriad regulations that govern research funding. I develop the training programs and help the instructors teach the courses effectively. I orchestrate the classes and enjoy facilitating the interchange between the instructors and the audience. This position grew out of my noticing in 1998 that a training program was needed in my office. I was told I could develop it, but it would have to be on my own time. I did it gladly—presented it, and the rest is history.

"To be or have what you've never had, you must be prepared to do what you've never done."   —*author unknown*

I've always admired the work of Mark Victor Hansen—and these words leaped out at me in one of his books that was a compilation of inspirational stories, ideas and words contributed by many. While these words didn't reach me until last year, they epitomize how I've been able to achieve what I have. To live these words, I had to be willing to do three things:

1) START. The easiest way to start an action is to allow yourself to,

2) MAKE MISTAKES. I've learned that mistakes are the stepping-stones to excellence. Being willing to make and embrace mistakes has probably been the single most important change I've made in my approach to life. And finally,

3) HONOR THE POWER OF FIVE MINUTES. Big blocks of time rarely appear—but you can move mountains— five minutes at a time.
So, in short, my formula for moving from a state of fear to one of confidence and living a full life is:

Find a need (including your own).
Visualize the need fulfilled.
START towards the fulfillment of the need—IMPERFECTLY—
FIVE MINUTES at a time.

In no time at all people will exclaim "WOW" as they watch you achieve *YOUR* dreams.

8

That Telephone Pole

by Teresa Watras Jones

I was taking a lunch break sitting in my dressing room. Deeply in thought, I was working on a difficult part in the play we were just rehearsing. Suddenly someone opened the door and yelled, "Teresa, there's a telephone call for you. *Hurry!*"

I jumped to my feet and ran! That was the time when Poland was at the peak of communist control. My country suffered years of constant deprivation of virtually everything in our lives. We had shortages of everything, except communist propaganda.

We had no private telephones, and business phones could never be used except in cases of real emergency. The phone network in the city before the war (World War II) was meager compared to today's means of communication. Indeed, the whole network was destroyed during the war and had never been properly repaired or improved in the years since. Very few people had private phones, and the waiting list for an installation was as long as fifteen years, depending on the nature of your work.

My husband and I were privileged because we both worked in the theater, and he was a well known celebrity, an actor, director, writer, singer, and professor in the National Academy of Acting. Our May-December marriage, with 27 years difference in our ages, had been blessed with the birth of our little boy, Martin, and our mutual interest and love of the theater arts.

At this time I was a promising young actress who had already had some success in both the theater and films. So, theoretically, we were entitled to have a new telephone, though we were not at the top of the list. Members of the communist party, government officials, doctors and police came before us.

After more than a year, we sent our third petition to the proper authorities for the installation of our desperately needed phone, but we got no response whatsoever. Hence, when I ran to answer this unexpected phone call, a thousand things raced through my head. Had something happened to little Martin, or my parents? Breathlessly, I took the receiver and said, "Hello?"

I couldn't believe my ears. Our petition for the phone had been accepted, and next Monday, which was our day off, the technicians would come at 8 a.m. to install it.

I was jumping for joy as I ran back to my rehearsal and shared the amazing news with my husband. We were both so excited and happy and could hardly wait for the next Monday.

Monday morning we got up very early, and were ready for the technicians long before 8 a.m. But at 8 a.m. nothing happened. No one showed up. No one came at 9 a.m. or 9:30 a.m., either. Little Martin was excited, asking over and over about the phone.

Finally, at about 10:30 a.m., the doorbell rang and everyone ran to the door, including our Irish setter, Lady, four-year old Martin, his nanny, my husband and me. When we opened the door, two very strange looking workers walked in, pulling a large canvas bag behind them. With them also came an overpowering smell of alcohol—Polish vodka. They could barely stand on their feet, and it was immediately obvious that they both were very drunk, a common problem among workers at that time.

Lady, like most dogs, despised the smell of alcohol, and growled. We quickly took her to Martin's room, leaving the rest of us standing in the hall trying to figure out what was going on.

One of the men was very tall, and his clothes were obviously too small and short on him, but he seemed quite clean. He wore a serious expression, and somberly tried to explain why they were so late. None of it made any sense to us.

The other man was quite short and also skinny, with everything too big on him, plus being very dirty. His drunken smile showed both rotten teeth and large gaps between them. He was saying, "Yes, yes," to everything his coworker was trying to explain. Then he would burst into loud laughing while wiping his mouth and runny nose with his already filthy sleeve, all the while drunkenly stamping his feet.

Little Martin was pulling my dress, asking "Mommy, mommy, why do they smell so bad?" Without answering, I asked Nanny, who had stood transfixed with an unbelieving expression, to take Martin to his room and keep him there.

The short man burst into laughter again, and suddenly became very personal. "Is she," he hollered, pointing at me, "your wife?" After a "Yes" from my husband, he said with another bellowing laugh, "I thought she was your daughter!" We tried to interrupt his insults, but then he asked my husband. "Was that boy your son?"

When told that he was, he bellowed another insult at me by saying, "Are you sure?" followed by still another guffaw.

My husband is usually a tactful and polite person, but he was now losing his patience. "You came to install a phone for us, so let's talk about it, now!" he said with a very firm tone.

Meanwhile, the very tall man had been trying to say something during this insulting exchange, but couldn't because he suddenly had developed a terrible hiccup and couldn't utter a word. He noticed the coffee cup in my hand, and desperately was trying to ask me for it. He sounded like, "Can I hic, hic, hic, have, hic, urp…"

Coffee was a luxury in Poland and unavailable in regular markets. We sometimes were able to get it on the black market, but at a very steep price. I thought coffee might sober them up. I went into the kitchen and made two strong cups of very hot coffee.

Back in the living room the tall man was still fighting his hiccups, while the short one had spread himself on an armchair and kept talking to his partner in a drunken, reflective mood.

"You see, Henry," he said, "they are artists; they will have a telephone and they have coffee, but what about us? Do we have anything like this?" Then he wiped his nose again on his sleeve.

While they drank their coffee, my husband sat with his head in his hands in desperation. The coffee was gone in no time. The tall man lost his hiccups but now asked somberly if he could have another cup of coffee. "It's a very small cup," he mumbled.

I refilled their cups as both of them began to tell us which play they had seen us in. They had apparently seen our play where I was playing the part of my husband's daughter. They were cousins, they said, and came from large families, and all of them loved the theater.

The coffee finally was working, and though they were making sense, we still hadn't learned anything about our phone installation.

My husband let go of his head, got up as if nothing had happened, and walked to the place where he told them he wanted the phone. In a stern tone he demanded, "Can you do it NOW?"

Henry, the tall one, now got up and brought the canvas bag full of phones in from the hall, picked out a phone from it, and put it on the small table where we had told him we wanted it.

He said, "Here's your phone, but we can't connect it."

Stunned, we both shouted, "What do you mean?"

Now they both started talking together, and for a moment we couldn't make out what they were trying to tell us. They finally told us that they couldn't connect a line to it. Not only that, but there were no telephone poles available anywhere now, and no one knew when there might be. Our neighborhood was new, and no one in the area had a phone yet, and it would take at least one pole to make a connection with the main line.

We were stunned and devastated as we sat listening to their story. After a brief silence, Henry whispered something to his cousin, and then said, "Maybe we can help get you that pole, but no one should know about it. I have another cousin who might be able to get one on the black market."

Now we knew their game. They were probably selling us the very pole that they already had for us. But we were not sure because of the uncertainty of everything in the country at that time.

We excused ourselves for a moment, went into the kitchen where we had a short talk, and decided to go ahead with it. We simply didn't want to deal with the authorities any longer. We returned and told them we'd buy their pole and needed it as soon as possible. Both of them were now visibly happy. Even Henry's usually somber face cleared up a bit.

Of course they wanted their money up front. Their price was very steep, but we gave them a small deposit, promising them the rest when the job was completed. We also got them six tickets to our theater, which they had asked for to see our new play.

We had to wait another whole month because it was still March and the ground was frozen. There was no excavating equipment available then, and the job had to be done manually when the ground was thawed out and soft.

Then one day a short time later at our theater, both of our phone workers appeared at our new show. They were dressed in their Sunday best, again full of good Polish vodka. They thanked us profusely and told us how much they liked our performance.

After another month or so, we became very happy as the proud owners of a working telephone—with its own pole right in front of our house. Martin was finally able to "talk to the pole," and we all had a connection with the rest of the world.

9

Of Horses and Bathtubs

by Janie Lee

O nce in a while you hear of great teachers and what they do to motivate their students, or overcome a momentary crisis. They become "Teacher of the Year." They win the "Crystal Apple" awards. They are recognized and honored throughout the school district. They are the greatest examples of the old saying, "When you're handed a lemon, you make lemonade."

Two of my sons were each blessed to have extraordinary instructors like this.

In 1973 there was a nationwide shortage of gasoline due to our unfortunate dependence on foreign suppliers of oil, and the attempt on the part of the "OPEC" oil cartel nations to cripple our transportation system and to control us where it hurts on the most personal level.

Whatever the reason, many of us still remember it well. You could fill your tank only on an every other day schedule depending on the last number on your license plate, whether it be even or odd. If it was an even numbered day, like January 2, only those who had last numbers 2, or 4, 6, 8, or 0 could line up around the block at the local gas station. Within a few hours, if you were lucky and they didn't run out of gas first, you might have the chance to buy enough gas to get to work. This was the oil company's solution to the dilemma, and all but the most ingenious were stuck with it.

Some people reacted in a most creative way. My son Douglas' teacher decided, since she owned a horse, to express her irritation with the system by riding it to school. After all that's exactly what teachers did a hundred years before. She apparently had no

Mustang
very low mileage

idea what impact this little demonstration of nineteenth century history would have on her students.

Well, her little mare became the celebrity of the school, so she decided to use it in a variety of ways. As a lesson plan, it became a visual aid for teaching animal anatomy; she wrote word problems in arithmetic with the horse involved where the students had to add, subtract, etc., as the horse performed certain tasks. She traveled certain distances, carried so much weight, etc.; as a reward, those who did their homework on time joined the list of those who could ride the pony around the school grounds, the coolest privilege imaginable.

Those who didn't do their work joined the list who washed, groomed and cleaned up messes, whether it was where it was tied up or anywhere it happened around the campus. These were not unpleasant chores for the most part. It just told everyone who was watching that you were the "dunce for a day."

The very presence of this handsome beast made celebrities out of her students, the envy of the rest of the student body. Compared to the rest of their schoolmates, the test scores from her classroom rose dramatically. Her rapport with the rest of the faculty members couldn't have been higher. When she had to give up horseback riding to school and return to driving an ordinary car as an ordinary teacher, it was a sad day indeed.

My other son Darryl had an equally innovative experience in one of his classrooms. His teacher didn't use a national disaster or a thousand pound pet to gain their attention. He simply used 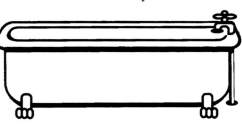 a *bathtub!* For some inexplicable reason, all of his students thought it was a great honor to spend the day propped up on pillows in this empty bathtub as a result of having the highest grade on the last test, turning in the best paper, having perfect attendance, etc.

They were always treated with the greatest deference, waited on, and given special privileges since it wasn't necessary for them to leave the tub, unless they wanted to or *had* to. This bathtub, like the horse, put the class under complete control of the teacher, and in a way the students loved and fought for the privilege. Again, the reputation for doing these things quickly spread throughout the school, and the upcoming students couldn't wait to get promoted in order to have the experience.

Another teacher set aside a table in the rear of the room for those who earned the role of "student for a day" where he or she would spend time making up work problem "adventures" with an unusual twist. These adventures had to be written with arithmetic challenges such as: distances traveled, heights climbed, or weight carried to tell the story. At the end of each adventure would be a blank for the missing word. She listed the possibilities for making words out of upside-down numbers, and they had to write their story so it would turn out with the "answer" as the inverted number. For example, when you turn the number 710 upside-down it becomes "OIL," and the number 7714 turns into "hILL." (See page 141 in the back of the book for 65 possibilities.)

Yet another, many times awarded "Teacher of the Year " honors, let all her students take the week off before the final exams to make up board games that required knowing the answers to the course they were studying in order to make up the game. Then, the day before the test, the games were passed around to the other students who played everyone else's game. They would all then grade each game (except their own) on a scale of 1-10, and the students with the top three totals didn't have to take the test.

In a school system that struggles with students who can't do the necessary work year in and year out, sometimes it's just a creative teacher doing simple things combined with a little bit of imagination that can make all the difference.

It would seem that the largest mass of disabled citizens is made up of unmotivated students who barely pass to the next level each year. These underachievers more often than not move on to a life of trouble and dependency. Let's hear it for the creative and caring teacher!

10

Blue Skies

by Bobby Miles

How many things do you still want to accomplish in your lifetime? Do you make goal lists? Dream lists? Things to do lists? If you do, then you're very much like me.

I look across the table at my stack of old journals. A rainbow of faint colors looks back at me. Within these faded covers, pages and pages of thoughts and feelings rest safely within worn bindings made secure by a variety of tape: scotch, masking, even some electrical. Each page is a living moment of my life as I make my way through the maze of time given to me.

Thoughts are things I have learned. And I have learned also they have a magical way of becoming a reality when I but take the time to trace them to paper. As water flows freely downhill, so too do my thoughts seek expansion. Feelings are translated into words, travel through my pen, and spill forth onto pages of white. Written words carry a power all their own, I have learned. A deep sigh escapes my chest as I sink back into my swivel chair. Dark brown eyes reach through the window, skyward, taking in the puffy whites moving ever so gently against the perfect sky of blue. A smile crinkles my eyes as I remember a day quite like this one. A little giggle renews the exuberance of that wonderful day when I did the most outrageous thing I have ever done!

It was on my list, in one of these old journals, not #1, but it was right up there with: • Travel to Africa • Ride a camel • Have a house by the sea • Join a sports car club • Attend the Bob Bonderant School of High Performance Driving • Take dance lessons • And—learn to play the drums. But going to jump school was the single most exciting adrenaline-raising time of my life. Excitement and extreme fear held hands on that day of my first jump. It began like this:

I was reading the list to my family of all these things I want

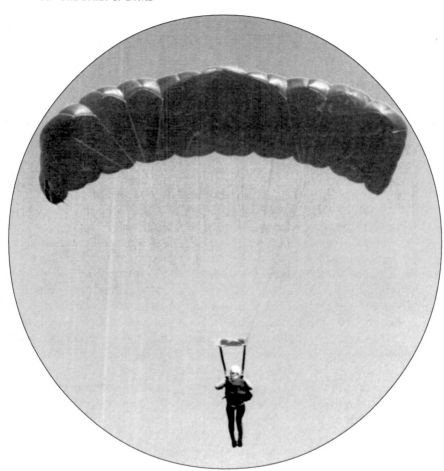

to experience in my life. My husband understood not, especially the one about jumping out of an airplane. My eighteen-year-old son laughed, and my daughter, who is much like me, joined my enthusiasm with rich vigor! She, twenty, and I, forty-two, soon began planning our attendance at the Antioch Jump School in Northern California.

The day began at 6 a.m. With nervous stomachs we drove from Sunnyvale to Fremont and on north to the Antioch Air Field where we were to learn the safety aspects of parachuting. The jumpmaster in charge, a burly military type, began his lecture. My brain scrambled to keep up. Three hours later we were strapped into a harness, and hoisted aloft; twenty students in full parachute harness, hung from the rafters of the huge instruction room.

On the far wall of the building loomed a large film screen. And the pictures began. Situations hazardous to our lives would flash before us and we were given three mighty seconds to demonstrate the correct measures. Demonstrating correctly could prove to save our lives tomorrow, on jump day. There were moments of brain freeze and tears, but in the end...we were ready. Tomorrow we would jump.

That night restlessness was my companion. I was nervous. I was scared. But this was something I so very much wanted to accomplish. I wanted to experience this wild thing. Every fiber of my being burned with unquestioning desire to do it. But fear led my parade.

Diane and I rode silently to the check-in. My husband, not too excited about all this, drove also in silence, though his 35mm was close at hand. We were issued our jump gear: helmet, goggles, two-way radio, a pair of lace-up boots size $8^1/2$ M, and parachute and harness.

"Okay this is it," said a little voice in my head and at once I started crying. The instructor, seeing my difficulty came to my side.

"I don't know if I can do this," I sobbed. "But I want to have done it!" I added. He took my hand and said, "We're going for a walk. I want you to tell me exactly what you are afraid of," he said in a voice more sincere than I expected.

I replied stupidly, "I'm afraid I'll land astraddle a barb-wire fence and get all tangled up!" "Look," he said, "at the size of this target. It's immense! This is what you'll be aiming for and you'll probably miss it...so what are your chances of hitting a fence that is only an inch wide?" Smiling, I dried my eyes and said to this gentle man, "Now, I'm ready."

The jump plane growled to a halt. The pilot nodded, and following the instructor we climbed in. Bare-bones it was. No seats, no doors, we sat Indian-style on the fuselage floor. Final instructions were given and jump order assigned. I was second, Diane was third. And with a deafening roar the plane bolted down the runway and soared skyward in big lazy circles increasing altitude with each turn. Cars, trees, and buildings became toy-like as we climbed toward clouds of white on blue.

First jumper out. I was up. My smile met Diane's as I stepped toward the opening. With left foot planted on the wing, my right hand held tightly to the doorpost. A monster wind grabbed my lips and stretched them into an ungodly shape. Props were cut and at the slap to my helmet…I jumped with all my strength…into…NOTHING!

My back arched, my arms and legs spread-eagled to avoid spin—and there I was, like a giant bird riding the wind. My parachute deployed and I shot straight up like a rocket. The adrenaline rush was so great, I shouted, "Look at me!—I did it!—Wooo-hooo!!"

I looked up and like the giant hand of God, my bright red chute canopied wide over my head. My lines were clear. I counted to five and again checked right, then left. Still all clear. I toggled right, I toggled left, and my direction changed with each pull. It was quiet. It was a blessing. It was heavenly…It was too short. The target growing large, I pulled both toggles to stall, and coming almost to a standstill my right boot touched down in a field of yellow wildflowers just short of the target.

What a day. My fingers touch gently my journals of old. Yes, they speak of me. Held captive within their pages is the essence of me. My list of goals prevails. Its length multiplies and I find myself enjoying the fact that the things I do were once brand new on my list of things to do. Will I jump again…that most outrageous thing I ever did? Only my list knows for sure…

ANTIOCH SPORT PARACHUTE CENTER
FIRST JUMP CERTIFICATE

THIS IS TO CERTIFY THAT *Bobby N. Miles* SUCCESSFULLY COMPLETED A STATIC LINE PARACHUTE JUMP AT THE ANTIOCH SPORT PARACHUTE CENTER, ANTIOCH, CA, ON THE *14th* DAY OF *April* IN THE YEAR *84*.

_____ D-12940
INSTRUCTOR

_____ D-8100
JUMPMASTER

11

Opportunity Is Always "At Hand"

by Dottie Walters, CSP

I once went to hear the very famous speaker and author Dr. Norman Vincent Peale. I went up to him after his presentation and handed him my new business card. What happened because of that moment changed my life and sent me all over the world! Here is how it happened.

The economy after World War II caused many people to be laid off work. My sweetheart, Bob Walters, returned after four years in the Marine Corps in the South Pacific. He was decorated for bravery after he went into the water at Tarawa under enemy machine gun fire to rescue wounded men in his platoon. As soon as Bob got back to Southern California we were married. We bought a GI-financed tract home, a dry-cleaning franchise, and had two beautiful babies. *Then the economy got worse!*

No one was in need of dry cleaning services. When Bob came home one night after knocking on doors all day asking for dry-cleaning orders, he sat and put his head in his hands. I had never seen him so down. He said he didn't know where he would be able to get the money for our house payment.

I told him I had an idea. If he could give me a couple of weeks, I thought I could help. I could see that he didn't believe there was anything I could do with two babies and no car. He had to take our old car to the dry-cleaning store each day. What could *I* do to help?

My father had abandoned my mother and me just as I was about to go to high school. I worked at many different jobs, giving my mother my checks during those four high school years. But then a wonderful thing happened. My English teacher asked the class to each choose a character from Charles Dickens' book *A Tale of Two Cities* and write about him. We were to write about where the character came from, and what had happened to the character next?

She read *my* story to the class!

My heart sailed around the room that day. Then she announced that I would be the Advertising Manager & Feature Editor for the Alhambra High School *Moor*, our school newspaper, for the term. I was thrilled!

I sold the ads on my lunch hour. However, the only time I had to work on my feature ideas was at night. The bakery I worked in was very quiet the last two hours of my eight-hour shift. Very few customers came in from 10 p.m. until midnight when my Mom came to pick me up. I wrote on the clean sides of partially soiled bakery bags after scrubbing the shelves, floors and the pans that held the bakery products.

Then the next morning I took my ad copy and articles into my journalism class. My teacher laughed, saying she had never had a student turn in stories and ads on bakery bags before.

One of my ideas was a comedy Advice to the Lovelorn column by a fictional "Professor O.G. Whataline." Everyone loved it, and no one guessed who wrote it (me). Another idea was a Shoppers' Column with paragraphs about different stores in each town. Each merchant paid to appear in that column, which I wrote. I sold the column spots as I sold the display ads to the same businesses.

The very same Shoppers' Column idea was my solution to paying our house payment. I approached the weekly *Baldwin Park Bulletin* newspaper and suggested I could write a Shoppers' Column right there in our chicken ranching town of Baldwin Park, California. Then it hit me I had no typewriter, no car, nor any typing paper!

What would I do with my two small children when I tried to sell the Shoppers' Column spaces? I had only one pair of shoes, and the soles were almost worn out. There were very few sidewalks in Baldwin Park.

The day my father left us, he had answered my mother's question about the cost of my going to college in a voice so loud all the neighbors could hear him—*"She does not need any college!"*

he yelled, because I was *"too dumb to be worth educating."*

My reaction to him was to turn to the public library where I read biographies of people of accomplishment and achievement. As I read about their dreams and how they overcame problems, I felt so close to them that I could hear their voices! Each famous person became my *"Friend of the Mind."*

Many years later, as I told this story about the voices in the books, a lady in my audience called out, "How dare you say those authors wrote their books for you! Most of them wrote their books long before you were born!"

I answered this way: "If they did not write them for my yearning, listening heart—who did they write them for?" My audience was silent for a moment and then gave me a standing ovation.

I told them again how I addressed the need to pay bills. I grabbed a pencil and made a list of what's needed to write a "Shoppers' Column" for a local newspaper. Each item needs a solution.

1. A typewriter
2. Typing paper
3. A way to take the children with me as I walked to town to sell my Shoppers' Column to the merchants.
4. My shoes were almost worn out. How could I fix them so that I could walk the two miles to town on the rocky streets with no sidewalks?

Since I didn't have any of these things, my heart sank. Then I remembered reading about Albert Einstein. In the book about him at the Baldwin Park Library, he said to me: "Stop fussing about problems, Dottie! INSTEAD— concentrate on SOLUTIONS!"

The minute the word "SOLUTIONS" popped up on the screen of my mind, I thought of my neighbor who had an old typewriter. I ran next door to her house and asked if I might borrow it for a couple of weeks. She was glad to loan it to me, and handed me a whole ream of typing paper! A whole REAM (500 sheets)! I was so glad to see that ream of paper I could hardly hold back my tears of appreciation.

After I wrote a sample column based on the ads in the sample newspaper, the *Bulletin* thrown on my front porch, I got our old baby stroller out of the garage and tried to put both of our children into it. In the old days they could fit on the one seat. They had grown! Then I realized, the oldest one could walk now.

Mr. Einstein again called out, "Solutions! SOLUTIONS!"
I cut pieces from a cardboard grocery carton to fit my shoes.
I made several extra sets. I put the first
set in my shoes, the rest in my purse.
Off we went!

The stroller wheel came off several
times, but I just took off my shoe and let
the old wheel have it with the heel!

When we reached town and found
the newspaper office, I saw on the door
a big sign "NO HELP WANTED!" My
heart hit the sidewalk, but my good
friend of the mind Ben Franklin (a journalist, too) whispered in
my ear: "Dottie, they do not have any money to hire you, so do
not ask for a job. Instead, become a customer for them! Buy their
ad space at wholesale and sell it at retail. That way you will not hurt
the newspaper's rates, and I promise you, you will have the money
for your house payment in two weeks."

The publisher let me have the first two columns on credit,
bless his heart. The merchants of Baldwin Park loved my
Shoppers' Column, and Ben Franklin's prediction came true. I
was able to pay that next house payment, and never missed one
from then on.

Then my girl friend bought two tickets for the Pasadena Civic
Auditorium where Dr. Norman Vincent Peale was to speak. He
was coming all the way from New York. She bought my ticket as
a gift. I was so excited. I had read every book at the Baldwin
Park Library about advertising, sales and journalism. And, I had
read Dr. Peale's *The Power of Positive Thinking*. He was like a
great friend cheering me on each time I picked up his books.

My girl friend was in a hurry to leave after Dr. Peale's
presentation, but I insisted on waiting in line to meet him in person
to thank him for writing his book—for me! I had just managed to
have my first business cards printed, so I pulled one out of my
purse and held it out to him when it was my turn in line. He not
only took it from me, he said, "Tell me about it." I quickly told
him about my "Friends of the Mind" and my Shoppers' Column
and how I was now able to make the house payment. He had the
kindest face I had ever seen. I held my breath wondering if he

would hand my card back to me. But no! He put it in his inside coat pocket. I thought, "He didn't throw me away!"

Then a week later Dr. Peale called me on the phone and asked if he could send me one of the interviewers from his *Guidepost Magazine* to see me so they could publish a story about me. They wanted to title it "What Can One Housewife Do?"

The interviewer came to see us, and at the end of her questions she asked me what else I was working on. I told her that I had read every book at our library by Dr. Peale, and also everything about advertising and sales. But I noticed there was no book by a woman, or for women in sales. The librarian tried to order books for me by women on these subjects from the county and state libraries, but there were none. Suddenly, I told her, in my mind I saw a book on an empty library shelf! The title: *Never Underestimate the Selling Power of a Woman.*

Then two weeks later Dr. Peale called me again! He said that he had been telling his audiences my story! He asked me who my publisher was. I had to tell him that 18 publishers had turned down my manuscript because they all agreed there were no women in sales in the United States.

Dr. Peale told me, "Dottie, tomorrow I have an appointment to talk to my publisher, Prentice Hall. I will take some of the copies of our *Guidepost Magazine* that featured your story and give them to my editor."

It was two days later that Prentice Hall called and asked for my manuscript! All the big Direct Sales companies were starting up: Amway, Mary Kay Cosmetics, Tupperware, and many more. The Great American Spirit of Enterprise was alive and well! Then Prentice Hall called to tell me that Tupperware planned to buy out the entire first edition of my *Never Underestimate the Selling Power of a Woman.* That led to my speaking to many Tupperware conventions and then other direct sales companies.

Then one day Prentice Hall called to tell me they had arranged for me to be on the popular TV show *What's My Line.* My husband and I would be flown to New York. Neither of us had ever been there before. What a thrilling trip! One of the things I wanted to do was to take the ship around the harbor so that I could see the Statue of Liberty as it must have looked to my grandfather as he sailed into New York.

None of the stars on the TV show guessed that the country girl from the chicken ranching town of Baldwin Park could possibly be the author of the first book in the whole world for women in sales. (Until that moment I did not realize it was the first. I thought there must be other books on the subject, but I just hadn't found them yet.)

The TV show had chosen two women to appear with me who looked something like me, about the same age, coloring, and height. The first was from Brooklyn. She had a heavy New York accent and sold girdles in a bargain basement. The second, a very refined lady, wore little white gloves, and ran a young ladies' "finishing school" in the South. The third person was me, the young housewife from the chicken ranching town in the West. We three each had to answer the same questions. One was "Who was the first American Advertising and Publicity man?" the other women gave names of well known people in those fields. When it was my turn, I said my great "Friend of the Mind," Benjamin Franklin. I won! So we were able to bring back the prize money, and the Baldwin Park Chamber of Commerce held a "Welcome Home Dottie" banquet in my honor.

If you're feeling left behind, or discouraged, may I suggest that you go to the library and meet my "Friends of the Mind." They are the greatest thinkers and doers in the world, just waiting for you in their books. Please tell them Dottie sends her love and heartfelt appreciation. Solving the problem of our house payment led me to speak all over the world, open more businesses that tie into the world of paid speaking, write other books, publish a large magazine, *Sharing Ideas*, about the world of paid speaking.

And, most of all, to have the great pleasure of people coming up to me carrying one of my books, all dog-eared and marked up, and USED WELL. Then they ask me to autograph it for them. I always tell them as I gladly do so, "I wrote it for *you*."

12

It's Her Business

by Patty Palmer Weckbaugh

S andy, one of my best friends in college had the opportunity
to establish a business after she married and moved from
California to Dallas, Texas. It was a giftware business
that required her to travel frequently to Western
Europe to deal with silver and porcelain craftsmen and manufacturers.

Twice a year she traveled to England and
Italy for silver items that she would then sell
from $10 upward to $50,000. Then she went
on to France where she bought hand-painted
porcelain. There her lack of acceptance as a
woman of business was something she was
forced to deal with.

France is famous for its prized porcelain, and
also as the land of the chauvinists. Being a woman and an American, she knew she already had two strikes against her. Nicholas
Chauvin became famous for his loyalty to Napoleon I, even long
after his hero was exiled in disgrace. His name has consequently
become synonymous with fierce loyalty to lost causes, such as
the myth of male superiority.

Sandy's shop was called the Silver Leopard, where she dis-
played all forms of imported, decorative silver and porcelain
giftware, specializing in hand-painted porcelain boxes. They came
from Limoges, a small French town whose craftsmen create this
exquisite giftware in ateliers, or designer's studios.

Her first trip there was in the mid-1980s, and she took another women with her. This proved to be very frustrating. Every-

where throughout the countryside that she needed to go to conduct business she was always dealing with men, who invariably considered these two women who claimed they had a business as just a couple of American housewives trying to shop for bargains.

So on the next trip she took her husband. It turned out he was the only person anyone wanted to deal with. He kept repeating to the Frenchmen, over and over again, "It's her business. Talk to her!" After several trips the locals finally got the idea, although a business*woman* still remained an amusing novelty to them.

Sandy's background throughout college and community plays was in theatre arts. She had always dreamed of one day becoming a professional stage or film director. But when she graduated from college in 1960 there were almost no female directors. She finally decided that after all it was perhaps just an "impossible dream."

Although she had no business classes in college, she began to hire business people on her staff when she started her venture into gift retailing and she learned from them.

Sandy

Within just a few years her Dallas store was grossing over two million a year.

Always involved in Dallas little theatre productions and community affairs over the years, she was asked to chair the Dallas Cotton Bowl Parade Committee. Whenever she had watched the parade on television, as a native Californian, she compared it not too favorably with Pasadena's Rose Parade. Since the major TV networks were going to be in Dallas to cover the parade before the nationally televised Cotton Bowl game, Sandy had confidence that she could make major improvements.

But the reaction to a *woman* taking over a major event in Texas was quite predictable. The Cotton Bowl Football Committee with whom she met was composed of ex-football players from the different universities in Texas. They had dealt in previous years with only other ex-athletes. They promptly dismissed her with the attitude of, "Why don't you just go away and 'do your little parade' and don't bother us." Sandy discovered that chauvinism was still alive and well down South.

But improve it she did, and successfully presided over the last two years of the parade before it was cancelled, much to her relief. It continued to be a thankless and frustrating job.

Though not a feminist, Sandy was used to overcoming these kinds of barriers and disappointments. When they were first married, her husband ran a large contracting firm that made important corporate installations worldwide. With Sandy's personable nature and marketable skills, she expressed her eagerness to be involved in *his* business. So she was given a job as a member of his marketing and advertising staff. Apparently, the board of directors felt it would be safe to put her in an out-of-the-way department and in a secondary role. Advertising turned out to be somewhat unchallenging in a construction company whose marketing efforts were quite narrow, depending on just a few major corporations for repeat business.

But partnership problems and other internal difficulties soon saw their business finances begin to slowly dissolve away into the hands of lawyers. After several years of court trials, they saw all of their business opportunities and assets disappearing as if in a puff of smoke.

It was then that the idea of the retail business began to develop in Sandy's mind, after she had done a considerable amount of market research. She interviewed and determined that several of the local businesses would be eager to support and cooperate with her intended venture after she showed how it could benefit them.

Most of them were more than willing to have a display case of her exquisite merchandise installed in the lobby of their establishments if she would share 50 percent of the retail profits with them. The exposure to such a large number of established local customers rapidly spread the Silver Leopard name and the quality of the giftware throughout Dallas without expensive advertising. She was successful almost from the start. Her little storefront enterprise eventually enlarged to nearly half a city block.

It was then the traditional roles in business started to reverse.

Her ex-president/CEO husband began to serve as the credibility factor during those first trips to France. Thanks to their strong marriage relationship and his considerable business acumen, they decided to integrate his skills into her business as it began to develop. He contributed his vision regarding their future marketing plans, and over the next several years he became her junior partner and business manager.

Nonetheless, he always made sure that everybody knew, for a fact, "it's *her* business!"

13

Against All Odds

by Ernie Weckbaugh

Hollywood actress Angel Harper, was born in the Harlem section of New York City. She is someone who has overcome all the odds and won. Being poor, black and female, she started with few advantages, if any. But in sharp contrast to her mother's generation, she was able to graduate from Cornell University, in the prestigious Ivy League, after attending on a full scholarship. She went to a Catholic high school, working as a dietary assistant to earn tuition.

She took no college-preparatory courses, convinced all along she would never go to college. But people at work said she should apply for a pre-med course in college under an equal opportunity program for minority students. So, when she found out that Cornell University in Ithaca, New York, offered one called COSEP, she applied.

Realizing she was probably at the end of the waiting list, Angel visited Cornell. One of the students directed her to the head of the COSEP Program. Very impressed with her interest in visiting the school, she arranged to put her up overnight.

Angel was so stunned by all the attention, she forgot to call her parents. When she didn't return home until the next day, she was in big trouble. But they quickly forgave her when they found out she had been accepted. "I was in shock. I had no idea how much that visit would help my chances," she said.

Unqualified, unprepared and without money, she bravely faced the challenge of heavy science courses and a lot of remedial work to make up for her lack of college-prep classes. She had been given a full scholarship as a pre-med student, which covered everything but meals and books. She worked summers to afford it. The turning point came when a friendly counselor made a remarkable suggestion when he found out she was struggling in her pre-med courses. He proposed that she take a double major, since she was consistently receiving an "A" in every one of her communications classes. She knew she would lose her scholarship if she dropped pre-med, where her grades were poor.

Angel took the advice, continued to pull top grades in her communication courses and was able to keep her grade average high enough to graduate. The counselor assured her, "If you graduate, no one will care what you studied or how well you did. It's okay to do what you like to do. The fact that you were able to graduate from Cornell says *everything* about you."

His continual encouragement, plus knowing that no one thought she would be accepted to the school in the first place, let alone graduate, kept her going and helped her get through.

Angel armed with her new Bachelor of Science degree in communication (radio and television production), moved to Washington, D.C. She successfully combined parallel careers in acting and business. Her communications background helped her land a job in sales and marketing. She received high recognition in corporate and feature films, commercial television and later as a writer. She authored a book titled *Master the Art of Cold Reading*.

In 1989 she moved again, this time to Los Angeles, where Hollywood welcomed her into the casts of such daytime dramas as *The Young and the Restless, Generations,* and *Santa Barbara*. Primetime opportunities followed with feature roles in *Anything But Love, Gabriel's Fire,* and *FBI—The Untold Stories*. They discovered her talent as a stand-up comedienne at The Comedy Store and The Improv which rounded out her performance career.

In addition to entertaining young people with her cartoon voiceovers on *Batman, Ghostbusters, Captain Planet,* and a leading role in *Kevin's Kitchen* on *Nickelodeon*, she's taken time to reach out to others whose beginnings mirror hers. She has done public service announcements against child abuse, and was the producer of a bilingual Latino play about families and AIDS titled *I Always Mean to Tell You...But*. She also serves as Southern California's Regional Director of Cornell's Black Alumni Association and is in the Endowment Program for "Women in Films." It is WIF's goal, as it is with Angel Harper, to encourage every young girl to seek her full potential.

14

The Bridge Builder

by Michael Fenlon, M.D.

Being five years old was not a good time in the life of my father, Ned Fenlon. It was during this time that *his* father, James, who was only 32, contracted a case of pneumonia which developed into tuberculosis. James fought a fire at his family's store in Hessel, Michigan, in the middle of a harsh winter night and fell gravely ill. As a result, when Ned was about five years old, he and his parents had to leave his two younger sisters and a brother and move from Hessel to Phoenix for his father's health. But his father became worse, and he died within a short time.

To complicate matters further, six-year-old Ned lost his voice. Polyps were discovered on his vocal chords as a result of a rare infection, and, although it might have easily been misdiagnosed as cancer, fortunately it was not. It affected his speech so that he could only whisper.

Returning to their family roots in Hessel, his mother, Anna, and his uncle took over the family grocery business known as The Fenlon Brothers Store. It had been rebuilt during their stay in Arizona. It was a very popular center in the little town and its reopening was warmly welcomed. In addition to Ned losing his voice, he also was severely nearsighted. A teacher later recommended glasses, and a whole new world of sight opened up to Ned. But in spite of these disabilities, Ned was given many adult responsibilities due to the loss of his father.

His mother continued the long-standing family tradition of welcoming members of the Ottawa and Chippewa Indian tribes as customers, always extending them full credit when the winters were harsh and money was scarce. She was so revered they gave her the Indian name of Chicadoque meaning "blue skies" because of her deep blue eyes. Their mutual respect and friendship grew, even to the family being invited to participate in special tribal ceremonies and events,

One day after he turned 12, the always-whispering Ned unexpectedly "shouted" a greeting to his friend Bill Blackbird in the native Indian tongue as Blackbird passed by the Fenlon home. Ned had to learn the language of the Chippewa and Ottawa tribes—the names of the store items, the produce and how to count. He needed to in order to work in the family store. It was a skill he still possessed into his 100s.

Blackbird was startled into a state of euphoria when he realized his young friend had suddenly regained his voice. He then suggested to the tribal elders that they declare it to be a special day of thanksgiving. Thus Ned was honored and celebrated for the recovery of his voice with tribal dancing and chanting in full costume. Their rituals of joy and gratitude were performed throughout that never-to-be-forgotten day in Ned's young life. His love for these special friends deepened into an enduring association all during his long and distinguished career.

One of his older cousins, whom he admired and who was a student at Notre Dame, talked to Ned about it. He needed to earn his way there, and so took a job working on the Carlisle estate.

The estate was in Mishawaka, Indiana, near South Bend. Carlisle was the head of the Studebaker Corporation, a great admirer of Notre Dame, and the Studebaker roadster he gave to Ned to use was one of the very few cars allowed on the Notre Dame campus at that time.

He graduated from Notre Dame in 1927, the year of the Four Horsemen of football fame and legend—Harry Studebaker, Jim Crowley, Elmer Layden and Don Miller. In his last year there, Ned studied in the law school and then pursued further training in the law at the University of St. Louis.

He also worked in various other jobs to support himself and earn tuition, including selling Fuller brushes door-to-door, working in Mertaugh's Chris-Craft boat sales in Hessel, working on boats and helping to pilot them up to Hessel from the Chris-Craft boat works in Algonac, Michigan, on the southern shores of Lake Huron and Lake St. Clair. About this time he was offered the position of running the speedboat owned by the Grand Hotel on Mackinaw Island. He jumped at the opportunity since it involved piloting a speedboat with a 250-horsepower V-8 engine, a real thrill for him to command such power.

One of the jobs for the Grand Hotel was piloting the hotel's speedboat across the lake to Mackinaw City to get the newest editions of the *Chicago Tribune* and race them back to Mackinaw Island for the guests at the hotel. The hotel's owners prided themselves on always providing guests with the most up-to-date news.

On these daily trips Ned had a habit of taking friends and their children with him as he sped across the water. This became the most exciting and popular part of his job. The children of an old family friend, Prentiss M. Brown, a U.S. Congressman and later Senator, were frequent guests on these speedboat rides. So later, when the job as an apprentice in Brown's new law office in St. Ignace became available, any competition for the position disappeared after Brown's children campaigned for their friend Ned.

As an apprentice with Brown's firm, he took the bar exam and passed it. All this happened between the years 1927 and 1933. Then Ned had a sudden opportunity to run for the state legislature. Their state representative committed suicide and, with less than two weeks remaining before the election, Ned mounted a tireless campaign and won.

Beginning at the age of 30, he served for six years in the Michigan Legislature from 1933 to 1939. He married my mother, Jane, that last year. Among the bills he sponsored were those to authorize the building of three very vital bridges: the Blue Water Bridge at Port Huron, Michigan to Sarnia, Ontario, Canada; the International Bridge at Sault Sainte Marie, Michigan, to Sault Sainte Marie (the "Soo"), Ontario, Canada; and the Mackinac Bridge (at the straits of Mackinac), St. Ignace, Michigan to Mackinaw City, Michigan.

These bridges would shorten automobile travel between the upper and lower peninsulas of Michigan and Canada to only a few minutes, whereas, before completion, it took the ferry time to be loaded with about 50 automobiles, and then take over 45 minutes to make each crossing. The waiting traffic was always jammed up for hours every morning and every evening.

Ned continued to work with the engineers from the San Francisco Golden Gate Bridge project, circa 1937, even after leaving the legislature. Ned was appointed prosecuting attorney for Mackinac county, where he worked from 1939 to 1943. Jane and

Ned moved to St. Ignace where I was born in 1940. Then they moved to open his new law office in Detroit—Brown, Fenlon & Babcock.

From there he was appointed a circuit judge in 1951 serving the three county area—Mackinac in the Upper Penincula, the Cheboygan and Emmet in the Lower Peninsula of Michigan until 1974. He moved his family from Detroit to Petoskey, all the time continuing his persistent pursuit of fundraising and bridge planning.

Finally, the Mackinac bridge projects began. The cost was a hundred million dollars (in pre-WWII dollars) from the early planning in 1935 in the legislature to its final fruition in 1954.

It took Ned Fenlon's tenacious leadership to make it happen. The enormous commercial benefits up and down the peninsulas, affecting the economies of Wisconsin, Canada, and other surrounding states, have been incalculable.

When Ned retired in 1974 at the age of 72, he could look back on a lifetime of achievement and the building of bridges, both structural and personal.

From a humble childhood, the loss of his father, mute and nearly blind in his later years, he created a century of life-long friendships that included the Chippewa and Ottawa Indian nations. He could often be found among the children of his Indian friends, teaching them of their culture and helping them keep their language alive.

Truly he became a legend in his own lifetime, revered and honored within his beloved Michigan and in his ancestral home in faraway Ireland.

His life has enriched the state of Michigan, the University of Notre Dame where he has been the longest-living alumnus, and the countless lives he has touched during the Twentieth Century.

15

A Chance Encounter

by Robert Kotler, M.D.

"Hey, Bob, how's that *special* patient of yours doing?" inquired Stephen Strum, M.D., an adult oncologist (cancer specialist). "Doing fine. Off chemotherapy; all is well," I happily replied.

Dr. Strum had collared me in a corridor at the hospital in which we were both practicing. The year was 1982. The patient, then a five-year-old, active little blond with emerald green eyes, had been off the cancer treatment for several months. She had even been a "poster girl" in a story titled "Childhood Cancers: A Brightening Picture," that ran in the National Cancer Institute's brochure *Decade of Discovery, Advances in Cancer Research 1971-1981*. In 1980, she had been diagnosed with acute lymphocytic leukemia, the most common childhood malignancy. At that time, thanks to spectacular leapfrog advances in medical science within one generation, the little patient stood an excellent chance of being cured. But no one could issue a 100% guarantee.

Dr. Strum said: "Hope you don't ever need this, but just in case, I recently read of a highly experimental new treatment that has been used in Germany. It's called the Berlin-Munich-Frankfurt Protocol. It has been used to treat adult lymphomas, but apparently was also successful as a treatment for recurrent leukemia. Keep it in mind."

I thanked him for his concern and scholarship, and we went our separate ways.

Months later, dark clouds arrived. On a routine blood count, the patient's prognosis had turned sour. The leukemia was back with a vengeance. The worst possible news, the prospects for survival had suddenly and drastically diminished. I needed to remind Dr. Strum of that hallway conversation months earlier, so I called and asked his advice; the patient's doctors had been extremely pessimistic about our little friend's chances and so were other experts. I had called one of the giants of childhood leukemia treatment at St. Jude's Children's Hospital in Memphis, Tennessee, where much of the original great work had been done in treating childhood leukemia. The doctor told me that she had a "10-30% chance of survival," down from 80% before the relapse. The odds were now reversed. The picture was no more optimistic from other major centers with long experience in treating childhood leukemia.

Strum, a specialist in adult cancer, but not experienced in childhood leukemia, understood the gloominess being voiced by the other specialists. He offered to help and I needed his help, because I was nearly paralyzed by the daunting prospect of suddenly researching a lethal disease far from my specialty.

I needed an "insider" to get some answers and to talk to the most knowledgeable physicians— and quickly! Leukemia cells double in number every three days.

Strum said, "I'll make a few calls and get back to you. A friend in need is a friend indeed." His calls included one to Sloan-Kettering in New York, one of the world's premier cancer centers. When he called back, Strum was quick and concise. "I spoke to a lot of people, but I think what I heard from Sloan–Kettering makes the most sense.

They have modified the Berlin-Frankfurt-Munich treatment. It's not quite as strong, but it is also less toxic, causing fewer deaths and complications. Given the situation, I think that's what you have to go with." I had my marching orders.

My wife and I then met face-to-face with the patient's doctors at the Children's Hospital of Los Angeles where she had been originally treated. The doctors there had a large fund of experience with all leukemias; their blood-disease clinic was the second largest in the country. I asked them if they were familiar with the modified Berlin-Frankfurt-Munich treatment, and they were.

The Sloan-Kettering modification, they said, appears promising but they didn't claim to have a large or long experience. They had reservations: it was so strong that they had lost some children early in the treatment because of complications, mainly infection. They reminded us that it was quite possible that she, too, could die from the treatment. We listened carefully and asked some more questions. There was no choice but to accept the risks, including death. Without newer, bolder treatment, in the face of the failure of standard treatment, there was no alternative. It was "all or nothing," and nothing makes no sense. It's a difficult thing to face your child's mortality, and it's agonizing to make decisions that include the possibility that the treatment you authorize—not the disease—might kill her. But with no reasonable alternative and knowing that children do have a leg up compared to adults in terms of resilience, we agreed to this new, experimental (now first-line, mainstream) and highly dangerous treatment.

The consent forms were voluminous; I hardly read them before signing. None of the caveats in this pile of lawyer-created papers could dissuade us. This was our only shot.

In the first several weeks the going had been very tough. The medications were so strong that our little friend's white blood count, the measure of the body's defense, was driven down to almost zero (normal is 4,000 minimum). The treatment not only destroys the "bad" leukemia cells, but also those "good" defensive and irreplaceable white cells. Now there were no soldiers to fend off an overwhelming attack by ever-present bacteria and /or fungi. All this time she was in the hospital and the doctors were as anxious as we were concerning the possibility of complications and death.

Finally, after ten long, anxious days, her doctor, a saint of a Welshman named Ken Williams, strode into her room dressed with a big smile to happily announce that Lauren's good white cell count had risen; her defense was building. Hopefully, soon, the first major danger point will have passed. We ordered in the patient's favorite Chinese food to celebrate.

After two weeks in the hospital, the little patient, now thinner of body and hair, was discharged home to continue the very intensive treatment with some of modern medicine's biggest (most toxic) guns.

Prior to her being discharged, the surgeons had installed an intravenous-like, plastic tube through her chest wall directly into the large vein to the heart so that she might receive medications through this portal.

The few precious and tiny veins in the hands and arms become shriveled and unusable from repeated blood drawings and harsh-on-the-veins chemotherapy, This miracle tube could also be the access port for the innumerable blood withdrawals for the frequent testing necessary to monitor the treatment. This spared the patient great discomfort and unpleasantness for the next two years.

That tube was a godsend! Blessed are its inventors, Doctors Broviac and Hickmann. Every night we sterilized the end of the externalized portion of that tube and then injected a medication to keep the blood from clotting within it, which would have rendered the tube useless.

After two years of treatment, the tube became infected and had to be removed. But, luckily, we were near the end of the protocol's timetable such that it would have been removed within a month or so anyway.

At that two-year mark, with the patient in remission (free of detectable disease), the doctors were guardedly optimistic. Less intense treatment continued for one more year, relying on fewer injections and more oral medications. At the end of the third year of treatment, having had five years of chemotherapy the first nine years of her life, the patient was scheduled for less frequent visits to the clinic. The words you always hope for: things are looking up!

That was in 1986. In January, 2004, we celebrated our daughter Lauren's 27th birthday. For all families, children's birthdays are special. In our family, every Lauren birthday is very special.

As I've often relived those difficult years, I've asked myself:

• *What if* we lived in another city and could not have known Dr. Strum, a unique physician whose legendary "literature digging" has made him a doctor's doctor?

• *What if* I had not run into Strum in the months prior to relapse and not had heard about the new treatment from Germany?

• *What if* Strum hadn't happened to remember that our daughter had leukemia and thus would have had no reason to share his recent discovery in the medical literature with me?

• *What if* I had forgotten that fortuitous Strum hallway conversation? I might have missed the opportunity to recruit him to help me do some investigative legwork I was incapable of doing, both scientifically and emotionally?

These chance occurrences in life, and the consequences thereof, are beyond understanding. Unexpected luck. Indeed, this particular chance encounter, a casual discussion in a hospital hallway, was a defining moment in my life. And, more importantly for our daughter, a conversation that was lifesaving.

16

Death Is Not the End

by Joyce Alexander M.A.

My father died just hours before the Jewish New Year, Rosh Hashanah. Now, every year when people wish me a happy New Year, it challenges my emotions. A holiday that was always a joyous experience is now bittersweet. While I accept and appreciate the good wishes from friends, the day now recalls one of the most tragic days of my life.

Just two days before my father died, my dear friend's father also passed away. I remember well my father telling me that day I would never know the pain of losing a parent until it happened to me. He also hoped I wouldn't know this type of pain for one hundred and twenty years. Then he gave me his best advice and told me to go sit with my friend and her mother and just listen to their thoughts with a loving heart.

Who knew that just two days later I would be calling upon the same friend to support me in my own father's death? Hours before Rosh Hashanah, and unaware my father had passed yet, I was driving down a canyon in Malibu, California, when the steering in my car suddenly went out. I managed to regain control of the car and felt something strange helping me at that precise moment. I had no idea what this astonishing external force was, but it had pulled me back to safety. I heard my father screaming from somewhere "You can't take my daughter and me from my wife on the same day!"

After I felt the car being pulled back from danger, I was able to drive down the canyon to the main road. I didn't know what had just happened, but I knew I needed to sit and take hold of my thoughts. I pulled a chair out from my trunk and sat in the sand staring out at the seemingly endless blue ocean.

After a few moments I felt this unexpected surge of incredible warmth rise up inside me, and for some reason I knew it was my father's spirit going through me. I felt as if it was telling me something, and I was filled with a sense of wonderment. I immediately knew I needed to get into my car and go to my parents' home. *This certainly had to be one of life's extraordinary experiences.*

I suddenly received a "911" alert on my pager from my parents, so I headed for their home. No one was there when I arrived, and shortly after my sister, who was at the hospital, called and told me our father had passed away. Moments later my brother arrived with his wife, also unaware of what had occurred. He looked into my eyes and asked what was wrong and I told him. He was in disbelief. We were all in disbelief. It was a huge SHOCK, because we had just seen our father days earlier.

We rushed to the hospital, found our mother and hugged her, all of us in shock. I went into my father's room with my brother and sister and then asked for some private time with my father. I stared at him, not understanding his leaving us, but finally accepting it. I now knew why I'd experienced this astonishing sense of his spirit filling me just a short time before. *It was his way of letting me know all would be okay in time.* I kissed his forehead, said my goodbye, and told him I would love and miss him forever. Then we located our other sister to tell her what had happened.

What helped me the most during this time was the love and support of my mother. I honestly don't know what I would have done without her. It was then I decided to make a CD on bereavement and write a book to help others go through this most difficult of times.

We don't often stop to think about the magnitude of emotions that erupt when we lose someone we love. Think for a moment about the tragedy that hit us all on 9/11. It struck most of us so deeply that we were unprepared for all the emotions that came forth from this horrific event. We need to prepare our loved ones for pain so they can better deal with major occurrences in life. I believe in miracles. I have good reasons for believing. I accept as truth, if you believe enough in yourself miracles can happen in even the most difficult of times. My cousin's dying wish was to go to the science museum before he died. However, he was not able to be around children because they often carried common colds and illnesses, which challenged his immune system weakened from leukemia. Therefore, everyone gave up on the possibility of his wish.

But I believe that human nature, when pushed to the test, will produce the great kindness and loving we all possess. With that thought in mind, I knew my cousin's wish had to be done within two weeks. I got in contact with the people at the museum, and they informed me the waiting period would be at least a few months. I expressed how we didn't have the luxury of time, and the doctors had given him only a few weeks to live. I just kept saying, *"If this was your cousin, what would you do? Please help me give him his dying wish."*

They finally went through all the channels, had an emergency meeting and agreed to open the museum for my cousin an hour earlier than usual so he could get there before the doors were open to the public. They even offered a tour guide. A limousine company offered to pick him and his family up without charge, and the driver offered his services, all out of the kindness of their hearts. My cousin's dying wish was met with kindness by those special, unforgettable angels.

Not all dreams can or will be achieved. Be passionate and do your best. Don't ever ever give up on yourself! Believe in yourself. It's all in you...believe me!

When it's my time to leave here, one of things I would like to have accomplished and be remembered for is living my life to its fullest, for helping others, and for making this planet a better place during my time here.

My goal is helping people get out of denial and empowering them to live *their* lives to the fullest. The only time I believe that happens is when we are powerful in every way and creating life strategies for success. I want to encourage everyone to take personal responsibility for their life while still alive, and plan for when they are gone. My book and CD are made to help people create a plan for almost every aspect of what needs to be done when the inevitable happens.

How can we live responsibly when we leave so much for the people we love to do after we're gone?

My system helps family and friends know what they want and how they can create it—step by step. I want to emphasize there are hidden miracles when we look for them, even in the most difficult of times. When my father died, the miracle was (without a doubt) that he saved my life. I felt him pull me back to safety when the steering went and I lost control. Before my cousin died, several people went out of their way and created the opportunity for him to have his last dream here on earth come true. If you look for them, you too will see there are miracles. The pain from such losses in our lives is great, but there are ways to deal with it so it doesn't absorb our whole being.

Most people don't have a plan when it comes to dealing with these occurrences. Some don't even hire a lawyer to explain the basic differences between a will and a trust. There are many choices a person can make that are never spoken about publicly. The reason for this is we live in a country where the environment is focused on youth. Hence, it creates an avoidance, almost a denial, about dealing with death. Though I have had to deal with several deaths of loved ones, no matter how many times one deals with such matters, it is never an easy subject to discuss. However, after losing my father, losing my best friend to AIDS without the ability of saying goodbye, my cousin to leukemia, another cousin to ovarian cancer, my uncle, my rabbis, my close friend to suicide, and more, I know that denial gets us nowhere.

Think about all the times you've been in denial. We think it will make us feel better to avoid such thoughts, but in the end we suffer more if we don't plan for the inevitable. Make your choices and plan your arrangements so that when the time comes, the ones you love and leave behind know your wishes. Make your plans, put them in writing, and make sure everyone who needs one gets a copy, then continue living. Enjoy your life, LIVE, dance and do what you love. We just never know how many days we have left. So live your life the way you choose to in every way!

My father's death was incredibly painful, and it started me on this path...to learn more about people's feeling. When such personal tragedies are endured, you can contact me at TheAlexanders Productions@yahoo.com.

I hope this story helps you on your journey in your time of bereavement. I have created a practical guide to help, step-by-step, when dealing with death. Everyone should empower their life now. My intention in writing this book is <u>to create</u> the most loving and natural opportunity for each and everyone of us to leave this planet with a complete and organized plan for our loved ones.

Because saying goodbye <u>should be the hardest thing to do</u>... once that part is done, we can truly <u>celebrate</u> our lives!

17

A Gift of Warmth

by Patsy Walker

On the first of October, 2004, we left for Cusco, Peru, to spend six weeks working with the deaf children of the orphanage called Centro Educative Especial Hogar, San Francisco de Asis. The people of GlobeAware made all the arrangements, including sending the film crew along to record all of our activities.

The Internet was used to organize a thorough search for anything to do with deafness. The producing organization was Concrete Pictures from Philadelphia, which specializes in documentaries. They discovered that our hearing-impaired daughter, Aimee, had been honored by the Young Artists Awards when she was featured in a film titled *How to Talk to a Person Who Can't Hear.* They found out about us through the lady who produced it, Christie Jenkins. Christie told them, because of Aimee, we all knew how to sign, and might be eager to participate. We might just be the ideal people for the project. The plight of these remote, forgotten people of the Andes Mountains was made worse due to many born deaf, the 10,000 to 15,000 foot altitude, and their extreme poverty.

The film was designed to be shown in nine episodes. Their purpose was to reveal the critical need in the Andes and elsewhere for volunteers to help these handicapped and destitute youth.

We almost declined to go at first. As a member of the Clinger Sister Quartet, I had been in show business all of my life, and I only wanted to be sure there would be no exploitation, just the chance to go to Peru, serve, and quietly do our part.

Our 23-year-old son Jamie and I went with the complete support of my wonderful husband, Cam. Jamie loves to learn new things and to experience new adventures, so he was eager to get involved. We joined the rest of the group at the airport in Cusco, after first landing in Lima. Eight volunteers had come to Peru from all over the world, among them Canada, England, and Hawaii. There the production company which made all this possible met us. Capturing our work on film created the needed financing for the trip.

Some of the faculty from Gallaudet University, which is famous for training deaf students, had come to Peru some 40 years before and established a sign language program. They combined an existing Peruvian style with American Sign Language with which we were familiar. Since about every fourth sign was different, it was challenging for Jamie and me at the beginning. We were the only volunteers who knew how to sign and had the responsibility to adjust to the new signing and then teach the others.

The interior of the orphanage had concrete floors and high concrete walls with tiny, broken windows near the ceiling, completing the appearance of a cement dungeon. Outside, behind a large gate, high up on the property, was a small fenced courtyard where they had planted a few trees.

We tried to expose the children to ideas regarding job experiences, since all but a few who stayed to work had to leave the orphanage when they reached eighteen. Of the nearly 80 children, 70 were deaf, many were mentally retarded, and only about five were perfectly normal. All were from families unable to care for them. They were either abandoned or deposited there from parents who were too poor or unable to cope with the child's disability.

Being so high in the Andes, these children seldom, if ever, experience warmth. Heat from a stove or fireplace was rare.

However, at least the children had food to eat and were able to obtain some schooling. What they missed were their homes and families, since the village where most of them came from was a steep four-day walk, and visits from a family member were often a year apart, if they were lucky.

My son Jamie Walker and three of the deaf Peruvian children of the San Francisco de Asis Orphanage are pictured here in their new clothes brought by volunteers.

While I was working with three of the deaf children, ages 4, 6 and 9, they kept running over to a man sitting in the corner to rub his sleeve, hands and face. They told us this was their father, whom they indicated by signing they had not seen for a long time. Their mother had to stay home with the other children and could not make the long trek down the mountain. When he saw I had a camera, I understood through his pantomime actions that he wanted me to take a picture of the three children to show their mother. She hadn't seen them in over two years. After I gave him the photo, he put it carefully in his inside coat pocket and kept patting it to show us he had put it next to his heart. Tears flowed freely when he had to leave.

We found a storage room filled with trash and cleaned it out and painted the walls white. But as an artist, I couldn't just leave it that way. So Jimbo, one of the other volunteers, and I covered the stark walls with scenes of the mountains and countrysides of Peru, which the children had seldom seen.

Few of the children knew how old they were and had never had a birthday party or *cumpleaños*. Jamie planned one for everybody. He, along with all of the volunteers, transformed the barren cement courtyard with piñatas, games, decorations, and a cake. The children's excitement was never greater, especially at the breaking of the piñata which showered the floor with candy and small toys.

After working in the orphanage several weeks, we were asked to go up the mountain to the small village of Salkatay, which was set around 15,000 feet. The houses were small, one-room buildings, with floors and walls of dirt and an open fire in the corner of each tiny room. The straw ceilings were jet-black due to soot from the fire. Many villagers had become ill over the years by breathing soot.

In the village large guinea pigs ran about freely. They were a source of food for the villagers. One of our projects was to build Lorena stoves for cooking and heating inside the homes. They were assembled from hand-made, 50-pound adobe bricks, hand-made mortar, and eucalyptus wood planks. This had to be done with very primitive, worn-out tools. The advantage was that these stoves were vented through the roof, eliminating the breathing in of deadly soot.

Another challenge was building wheelchairs by assembling kits with wheels and plastic chairs. Most of the volunteers were women, and it was the most physically exhausting labor I've ever done.

Back at the orphanage, a lady came who was writing an article for an American magazine. She had several "stock" questions for me to ask the children through sign language. Her first question was, "If you could meet your favorite 'Superstar' who would it be?" The first child signed back to me, "Mama and Papa." When I told the lady reporter, she said, "No, no, they don't understand. They can have anyone they wish." I told her, "Yes they do understand, and these are the heroes they want in their lives."

Then she asked, "What is their most horrible nightmare?" The overwhelming answer from the children was, "Leaving Mama and Papa, and my home."

Again the lady said, "No, no, they don't understand the question." Again I answered her with tears in my eyes, "Yes they do. That truly is their most horrible nightmare. Their greatest *dream* would be that they were loved by their parents and cherished in a home, no matter how impoverished the surroundings."

18

The Carney Kid

by Kenneth Kahn, Esq.

As a Los Angeles criminal defense attorney, I have poignant memories of my twisted youth as the oldest child of parents who were caught up in drug abuse. They were small-time carnival hustlers and petty thieves who lived like gypsies and taught their three children the tricks of carnival life.

The Projects

Nothing in my 12 years prepared me for the events leading to our family's move into the L.A. County Housing Projects in the spring of l954.

We had been living on Alsace Avenue, a palm-lined street in a middle-class neighborhood known as West Adams for about five years when a broken-down municipal moving van pulled up to collect our aging furniture that had been unceremoniously dumped onto the front lawn by the Sheriff's eviction squad a few hours earlier. Curious neighbors watched as two burly, unshaven movers clad in dirty overalls flung our few personal belongings into the back of the truck.

I only vaguely understood why we were being thrown out. Apparently, it had something to do with l0 months of unpaid rent,

My dad, Barry, was talking to the movers while Mom scrambled about trying to minimize the damage to our property. She carried my infant sister, Cookie, in one arm while directing operations with the other. The two moving guys largely ignored her.

The baby was crying and squirming in Mom's arms. She had arrived only two weeks earlier after being released from County General Hospital where she had been born two months prematurely. One of our neighbor ladies, Mrs. Spitzer, who was visibly upset, offered to hold her. Mom readily accepted, then dashed back into our house to make a final inspection. On her return, she had our family pet, a duck named Squeeky Mae under one arm and the cage in which she slept under the other. The duck, which I had brought home from the California State Fair in Sacramento two years earlier, quacked in alarm, as though she understood that all was not well.

My eight year-old brother, Ricki, stood by my side as we watched the last of the family's belongings being tossed onto the truck bed. "Why are they taking our stuff?" Ricki asked. "Did we sell it to them?" I put my arm around him and tried to reassure him, "Don't worry. We're just moving to a new house. It's still our stuff." I put on my bravest face because he looked up to me, but I was pretty shaken myself. I had no idea what was going on, but I knew it was nothing to celebrate.

When they were finished, the moving van driver announced, "We're done. Let's get outta here!"

Mom retrieved Cookie from Mrs. Spitzer, who was now crying openly, then handed the baby up to my brother who sat dazedly on our tattered sofa in the back of the truck. Mom climbed aboard and sat next to him. She held the baby while Ricki held the duck.

Dad and I headed toward his '39 Plymouth and started to get in when our former landlord, Mr. Wells, appeared on the front porch of the house and began to yell at us. "You low-life Jew bastards cheated me out of a year's rent. I hope you all rot in hell!"

Dad got out from behind the wheel, leaned over the hood of the car, and shouted back, "Everyone knows you left the country because you killed your wife. You belong in jail for murder!" Dad was referring to the local rumor that was going around the neighborhood, spread by nosey housewives.

Wells shot straight upright as though he had been struck by an electric cattle prod. His face was beet red with rage, in contrast to his shock of white hair. "I know what you do," he screamed. "You're nothing but a dirty DOPE FIEND!"

The accusation rocked through my body with the certainty of its truth. A hundred unanswered questions I had while growing up were suddenly washed away. The strange visitors coming to the house in the middle of the night, the mysterious meetings in the bathroom, the acrid odors left in their wake now made perfect sense. I had seen movies in school about the "dope" underworld, and had been properly frightened. But this was the first time anyone had ever used the dreaded epithet "dope fiend" in my presence.

Wells' accusation was virtually confirmed when Dad flew into a maniacal rage and began to stomp menacingly across the front lawn towards Wells. He was seething and looking to inflict great bodily damage on the man. Instinctively, I realized that a nasty confrontation would worsen an already disastrous situation. Having played a lot of sandlot football in my day, I lunged for him and managed to tackle one leg as he strode across the yard. I failed to bring him down, instead holding on for dear life as he dragged me along with him towards Wells. "Don't do it, Dad," I pleaded. "It's not worth it. Let's just go."

The crowd of onlookers had grown in anticipation of seeing a good fistfight. This kind of drama was not a common occurrence in our peaceful, middle-class neighborhood and would have made for some lively dinner conversation.

Dad's progress was slowed considerably by my dead weight on his lower leg. Finally, he looked down at me and realized that I was not about to release my grip. He relented and said, "O.K. You can let go. I don't need a probation violation anyway. Let's get the hell out of here."

We got back into the Plymouth and tailed the moving van dutifully as it turned east on Adams Boulevard, heading toward downtown Los Angeles. I was still thinking about the "dope fiend" comment and what it meant for my life. I barely noticed the deteriorating quality of the buildings as we veered east through the city.

When I came out of my worrying for a moment, my mouth dropped. All around me were dilapidated structures with "For Rent" signs posted on their broken windows. Staggering winos inhabited the shadows between vacant stores. I wondered where we were going.

The "dope fiend" words rang in my head. I could not shake them loose. The images in the films shown at school just did not mesh with the life I had known with my parents.

The moving van spewed a steady stream of black exhaust that clouded the windshield of the Plymouth and forced us to roll up the windows. As we passed through downtown, I began to wonder just how bad neighborhoods could get. The signs on the streets were no longer in English. *Llantas usadas*, read one in front of a dirt-paved parking lot filled with rows of used tires (llantas) piled six feet high.

When I finally cracked the car window to get some air, I noticed foreign aromas that caused me to wrinkle my nose. The stench of unwashed streets, together with the mixed smell of garbage and cooking grease, created a nasty odor. The people on the streets were shabbily dressed. Many gathered around vending carts selling some kind of unfamiliar food.

The events of the day were beginning to settle on me. I was having trouble sorting it all out. I wondered how long it would take to reach our destination, but now I hoped it wouldn't be too soon, given that I had not seen a single place that seemed remotely livable since we left our happy home in Ozzie & Harriet land.

The sun was beginning to set, and the moving van led us into a concrete and brick fortress known as "public housing." As we descended the Lancaster Street hill into the Ramona Gardens Housing Projects, my nervousness turned to fear.

The crumbling walls of a dilapidated single-story building with cracking paint were covered with graffiti. *"Hazard Grande, con safos,"* one read. I didn't have a clue what it meant, but I guessed it didn't translate as, "Welcome little Jewish kid from the Westside."

At the entrance to the projects, at the northeast corner of Lancaster and Murchison, stood a cluster of tough-looking black guys, some pretending to spar with each other. Others were mimicking the words of a song blaring from a radio perched on a junked car.

On the opposite corner was an equally rough-looking gathering of young Mexicans. I studied them with concern as we drove by. They wore khaki pants and Pendleton shirts buttoned at the top. I could hear them speaking Spanish as they squatted in a semicircle, smoking cigarettes.

None of these people resembled my playmates on Alsace Ave. It was hard to imagine playing ball in the street with them. It was hard to imagine talking to them or becoming friends. It was hard to imagine I was here at all. Although I had always been a pretty outgoing kid, I was in no great rush to meet them.

At last, the wobbly old moving van pulled into a parking lot behind 1342 Crusado Lane, one of a row of low-slung apartments that resembled a second-class military housing barracks, only not as nice. The driver of the van jumped out, approached the window on Dad's side of the car and tersely said, "You're HOME."

Mom lowered herself from the back of the van and Ricki handed her the baby before jumping down himself. He reached back up to get the duck, which began squawking. Ricki held her tight to comfort her, but the quacking got louder. Dad and I exited his car and headed for the rear door of the apartment, where he used a key to unlock it.

As the door swung open, we were greeted by the sight of thousands of cockroaches scurrying about the kitchen floor. I had never seen a roach before and was not ready for the panorama of insects unfolding in front of me. I jumped back, accidentally giving my little brother a good whack on the head, nearly knocking him down.

Mom craned her neck in the doorway to get a glimpse of the interior, then recoiled in horror. "Get me out of here," she demanded. "Get me out of here right now!" She covered the baby's eyes and retreated to the Plymouth. "I'll never set foot in there," she stated in no uncertain terms.

Dad was able to find a fallen-down motel behind a taco stand near the corner of Marengo and Soto streets, not too far from the projects. We had stayed in seedy motels before while traveling on the road for Dad's carnival business, but this place was an all-time low. It gave new meaning to the word "dump."

That night, all five of us slept in the same bed, clutching each other for reassurance. No one got much sleep.

Fast Forward to '58

Ray Lopez, my favorite teacher during my time at Lincoln High, plain and simple *changed my life!* Just to see an individual with such energy, devotion, and good will was a revelation in itself. I had no idea people could be like that. Toward the end of my junior year, I was approached by some students who suggested I run for student body president for the following school year. I'd been elected to the school senate, the first official office I had ever held in my life. They encouraged me to open a full-on campaign.

The day of the election, I was all nerves. I sat in classes, not hearing a single word the teachers said. I began to regret having run for office at all. It wasn't really my idea, and I feared the embarrassment of being trounced. In addition to all of my other insecurities, I was aware that Lincoln had never elected a student body president from the projects. By the end of the school day, I was an emotional mess.

That afternoon, during fifth period, a messenger came into our social studies class and handed a note to the teacher. "Class, I have the results of the student body elections for officers for next year," she said. I held my breath as she read the victors for the various offices.

At last she said, "And our student body president for 1958 is...KENNY KAHN!" She smiled broadly at me and invited me to stand and accept a rousing round of applause from my classmates. The blood rushed to my head as I rose.

It was incomprehensible. I had WON! The reality was overwhelming. Then she continued, "Kenny received a majority of votes in every homeroom in school. This is a first in Lincoln history." I was mobbed by kids slapping me on the back and wishing me good luck.

The weeks leading up to my graduation in 1958 were filled with excitement. It was hard to believe that my years at Lincoln were about to come to an end. While I looked forward to moving on to college, leaving my beloved high school was a terrible loss. In all my years in the projects, Abraham Lincoln High School was the bright spot in my universe.

No matter how bad things got at home or how desperately broke we were, the beautiful campus offered a safe haven. I was more at home there than I was in my own bed. For five years, it had been my savior, my security blanket, and I was not ready to leave it.

The school auditorium was filled to overflowing. Backstage, there was a last-minute dash to prepare for our final production. Ray Lopez was a blur of activity. I realized just how much I was going to miss this remarkable man, and I gave him a big hug.

I peeked out from behind the curtain to check the audience. Mom was seated in the front row with my brother and sister. She was animated, talking to everyone around her. She looked like a different person. She had quit drugs "cold turkey," a huge challenge for her. Now she was beginning to experience a rebirth. I was very proud of her.

"I would like to begin our program," I said to everyone, "by turning the mike over to our class sponsor and guiding light, Mr. Raymond Lopez." He came on stage, thanked me and began the formal proceedings. He acknowledged our class as being "special," then turned the show over to the principal who introduced the speakers.

The rest of the program turned into a vague cloud for me. I remember receiving a gold plaque and a small scholarship from the Bank of America for excellence in Liberal Arts. Everything else went off smoothly until the principal announced, "And now we have a highly unusual award to present. It has not been awarded to a Lincoln High School student in many years. It is my pleasure to introduce the presenter for the American Legion 'Boy of the Year' Award."

In a matter of moments, the legionnaire reached into an envelope and withdrew a document. "And this year's award goes to... KENNY KAHN. Kenny, please come forward." The crowd rose to its feet as one and burst into a deafening applause. All I could see was Mom accepting backslaps and hugs from those nearby. She was beaming.

So was I.

19

An Unwanted Journey

by Regina Leeds

"Your doctor called. He needs to speak to you." It was July 27, 2002, the day after a D&C to remove a polyp from my uterus. It had caused heavy bleeding and the most severe cramping I had ever experienced for seven months. The nurses at Cedars Sinai Outpatient Center in Los Angeles urged me not to go home alone, so I had spent the night at my friend Anne's house in the Marina. Her tiny Maltese Snowy had been my nurse from the moment we walked in the door. When Annie dropped me off at my home the next day, Snowy did something she'd never done before or since. She cried for me. I think Snowy knew.

My neighbor and friend Todd is my trusted dog-sitter. He had taken my ob/gyn's phone call that morning. I called my doctor's service thinking he must have good news for me. Why else would he call me on a Saturday? I was patched through to him immediately. "I am sorry, Regina, it's cancer."

"OK," I said, instantly sliding into shock. "What do we do now?" As soon as possible, I would be scheduled for a total abdominal hysterectomy with staging for cancer. He would ask Dr. Ronald Leuchter, a renowned gynecological oncologist to take my case. I was entering a world I knew very little about. I had to quickly learn a new vocabulary. And I somehow had to wrap my mind around a reality I did not want to accept.

I hung up the phone not knowing what to do. The first phone call I made was to my best friend, Susie. We have been best friends for over 20 years. Just a month before, she had buried her mother after a long and difficult battle with Alzheimer's. Susie had moved to Phoenix three years before to help take care of her mother. She had just lost her job and was winding up her last weeks at the company. How could I add to her burdens? On the other hand, how could I get through this without her?

Before the day ended, Susie had left her five-year-old daughter in the care of her sister and was in my living room. We talked. We wept together. Slowly, without realizing it was a plan, we began to devise a way to handle this experience. Susie and I are different in many ways. We share, however, a similar approach to life. We can deal with anything if we understand it and have a plan of attack. Gradually over the next 48 hours, the team of friends who would help me make this journey began to take shape. I have singled out one for you to meet now.

Grace and Dignity

In the beginning, my prayer was always the same. It was the prayer Jesus is said to have uttered in the Garden of Gethsemane, the night before his crucifixion. "Lord, let this cup pass from me. But Thy will, not mine, be done." Friends wanted to know if I asked "Why me?" I was quick to point out that I had instantly and consistently asked a different question: "Why *not* me?"

Listening to the news became a new experience for me. The Buddhists were right: suffering is a part of the human condition. I identified with each mother who lost a child, each soldier who died in battle, every victim of crime and every abandoned animal who suffered at the hands of the cruel. It did not matter their race, creed, or location. I was not exempt.

I was part of this fabric of life. As time passed, and the treatments were laid before me, my prayer became an even simpler one: "Lord, I have no idea how I can do the things You have set before me. All I ask is that, each step along the way, You give me the courage to act with grace and dignity."

Lying on the gurney outside the OR before my hysterectomy, I shook with fear. A sweet male nurse assured me: "Honey, everyone is afraid!" I told myself there would be no point in jumping up and running through the halls of Cedars. My situation was clear: have the surgery or prepare to die. You can't leave cancer growing inside you and expect any other result.

A Prayer Is Answered

"Grace and dignity" were repeated over and over in my head like an ancient mantra. And then, as I noted every single step of the way, an angel appeared to help me. Dr. Omar Durra, the anesthesiologist who had assisted at my D&C the previous month, walked over to my side. "I remember you!" he said, not realizing I had requested him again. Dr. Durra is a young man with an aura of compassion and a gentle manner far beyond his years. I felt safe with him.

As he approached he asked softly, "How do you feel?" I replied honestly. "Oh, basically, I am terrified." Suddenly something prompted me to ask Dr. Durra where he was from. He said: "I told you last time. I am from Jordan." "No, Doctor, you didn't tell me that. I would have remembered. You see my mother was Lebanese." Now Dr. Durra looked at me differently. He smiled sweetly, patted my hand and said: "Now I know why you are so pretty. All Lebanese girls are pretty!" I laughed in spite of my fear. "Don't worry," he said, "I am going to take good care of you."

Now Dr. Durra moved to the other side of the gurney. He began looking for my vein. He would start the IV here in the waiting area before we were called into the OR. The head nurse came over and scolded him. "Doctor, they are ready for her. You can do that in the OR." "No," said my protector, "I am going to do it here." Dr. Durra is one of those rare practitioners who can put an IV needle into your vein without any pain. He took my hand and said: "Remember now. I promise to take good care of you." The next thing I knew, I was being wheeled back into my room. Without saying a word, Dr. Durra spared me the OR experience.

Shortly after surgery when chemotherapy loomed on the horizon, I was connected to a cancer survivor by phone. I never met her. Indeed I do not remember her name. She said something to me, however, that I never forgot. "Right now you think cancer is doing something to you. One day you will see that it is doing things through you and for you." I didn't understand at the time but now I do. I wouldn't have volunteered for the experience and I hope I never have to grapple with cancer again. I can in no way deny, however, that it changed my life for the good and made me a better person.

I came to know that angels exist. I was not singled out for God's mercy. Some of my helpers were friends who responded to the call.

Others, like Dr. Durra, seemed to be sent by an unseen hand that guided and protected me each step of the way. The point is simple: open your mind and heart and you will see that loving spirits populate this world. Perhaps the trick is not to be open to finding them, but rather to strive to be one.

20

A Trip Down the Memory Train

by Michael Varma

The last words I spoke to him were from one of his secret poems, a modified version of Psalm 23:

*"My shepherd is the Lord;
I shall not want.*

*I fear no evil though
I walk into the dark of death.*

*For You are near;
Your rod and staff will comfort me."*

We were fortunate because we used every opportunity to share our thoughts, ideas, and plans for the future, both his and mine. One of our chats turned into a secret adventure that almost never came to be.

It began like a *Tale of Two Cities* by Charles Dickens—"It was the best of times, it was the worst of times." The best of times was when I was extremely nervous, to the point of having an anxiety attack. In mid-1997 I was about to ask a Southern Gentleman for his daughter's hand in marriage. Although we had corresponded, this was the first time I was going to meet him in person. So I was understandably nervous, but one look at Barbara and love filled my soul providing me courage and strength to steady my words.

We went to eat at Mimi's Café, to break bread the Californian way and chat over dinner. While waiting for our food to be delivered to our table, Mr. Neal proceeded to interview and size me up in his polite Southern manner.

After about the first dozen questions he asked me, "Michael, do you know Barbara's middle name?"

I promptly replied, "Yes sir, I do. Her middle name is the perfect complement to my middle name. Your daughter's full name is Barbara *Jane* Neal."

Fully capturing his interest, he inquired, "And your middle name?"

I paused, looked at him with my best poker face and said, "Tarzan."

A smile lit up his face a mere second before he let out a hearty laugh. It was an uncontrollable belly chortle that shook his entire body and brightened the room. It was a good laugh.

Mr. Neal turned to his daughter and said with his slight Southern drawl, "Now Barbara, he's ah keeper."

Those memorable moments will forever be etched on my mind.

Then followed the worst of times. Several weeks later the vibrant Mr. Neal was in the hospital with an unknown ailment. After a battery of tests and exploratory surgery, we gathered to receive the news. The life shattering diagnosis was cancer. Specifically, pancreatic cancer in stage three of its four cycles. What do you do with incurable news like that? How do you conduct yourself in such a lethal situation? We all took our cues from Mr. Neal who chose to face every day with 100-percent dignity and grace.

Our wedding plans continued with Mr. Neal walking his daughter down the aisle to place her hand in mine. Barbara and I would visit Mr. and Mrs. Neal frequently. We all would go out to dinner, take a Sunday drive around town, or walk along Laguna Beach.

I remember one Sunday afternoon when we all were relaxing and chatting in the living room. Barbara and Mrs. Neal were sitting on the couch across the room. Mr. Neal was sitting in his comfortable blue lazy boy recliner with me just to his right.

While Barbara and her Mom were engaged in an animated conversation, Mr. Neal handed me a newspaper clipping and asked me in a low secretive voice, "What do you think about that?"

I read the headline: "Model Train Convention Pulls into the Anaheim Station." The article stated, "Doors open Saturday from 9 a.m. to 6 p.m." I looked up at Mr. Neal to see another little boy smiling back at me.

"Michael, why don't we attend—just the two of us. It will be our little secret," he said conspiratorially.

I nodded my yes, understanding he wanted to escape and have some solitude away from the doctors, nurses, and stringent chemotherapy regimen. I whispered, "I'll pick you up at 8 a.m."

I could hardly wait. Father and son-in-law bonding time around the holy grail of boyhood dreams—model trains. I arrived Saturday morning ready with boundless enthusiasm.

Unfortunately, Mr. Neal was not. When he answered the door, it was clear the cancer treatments and powerful medication had completely drained his energy.

The true Southern Gentleman returned as he summoned his strength to say, "Michael, I'm feeling a little under the weather. Maybe we can go another time," and he headed back to bed at eight o'clock in the morning.

Our secret adventure was effectively canceled, the great escape thwarted by the reality of the situation. I returned to my car feeling hopeless and helpless.

While driving back home I had an idea. I was not helpless and I could change the dismal circumstances. I pulled into the nearest supermarket and purchased six disposable cameras, then drove directly to the Anaheim Convention Center. I parked, took the cameras out of their boxes and started taking pictures. I took photos from the parking lot, to the entrance, and throughout the entire Model Train Convention. I stopped often to ask many questions.

"How long did it take for you to set up your display?" "What kind of train is that?" "Is that real smoke coming out of the engine?"

After a quick stop at the one-hour photo shop, I was back at the house by the late afternoon. Mr. Neal was reposing in his familiar blue recliner, and I pulled up a chair to sit next to him.

For the next few hours we took a trip down the memory train. I shared every picture and described in the greatest detail possible everything I witnessed and learned. The moment his eyes entered the model train convention center, he transformed into a healthy young boy with a smile permanently fixed on his face. He laughed with happiness and delight as he looked at every picture. It was a good laugh.

That is our little secret that almost never came to be. And why have I decided to share this secret? Because it's not a secret at all. It *was* and *is* a choice. The same choice we all have, at all times. The choice to be happy, or not. The choice to take action, or not.

Most importantly the choice is entirely yours.

21

Doom & Gloomers...Sorry

by William Atwood, Ed.D.

Maybe the doom and gloom crowd is right. The optimists that surround us are just living in a fantasy world that says everything is going to be O.K.

The daily news in newspapers and on electronic media tells us constantly of the problems facing this state, nation and the world. They say the economy is not doing well, oil is at an all-time high, there is lying in government. People are homeless, there's no control of our borders, the Middle East is still at war, drugs are destroying a generation of Americans, the public schools are in a sorry state, and individual morality as portrayed on popular television shows is at an all-time low. In short, we have made a mess of things. Ah, for the good old days.

There are some among us that see the glass half full. Others see it as half empty. There are rocks along the pathway of our lives. We can view those rocks as stepping stones or roadblocks. The choice is ours.

I think things are rather rosy right now. In fact, I think these are great times. The economy is the strongest in the history of the world. Inflation is quite low at this time. All we need to do is remember back a few administrations and recall double-digit inflation; 10-17 percent price increases annually were very difficult to deal with. We got that under control, thanks to the work of some great thinkers and the changes that business folks made in how the economy was running.

The stock market was at the 11,000 Dow Jones mark when the terrorists hit the twin towers in 2001, and stocks took a tumble. Our weakened economy was supposed to plunge the entire world into financial chaos.

Wait a sec! The Dow moved above 12,000 in 2007, along with the Chinese, Japanese and other stock markets around the world which are booming! When I was in school the Dow Jones average was in the 700s. Oops, we did well there too.

Lying in the government is disappointing, yes. New? I think not. Both parties have historically blamed each other. Both seem shocked and appalled when someone in the other party is caught telling a lie. Well, they do! The press feeds on this kind of story and makes it last as long as possible.

The sorry state of affairs is that we seem to ignore it, especially when many come to their defense after they've done it. Presidents have lied to us in the past. We don't need to panic or accept it. We can just vote them out.

Pundits tell us there are over 5 million folks who are homeless. You don't have to buy it. We would be stepping all over them in the streets. It's all in how they count them. I know of some folks who, by choice, live with their parent or parents. It is a good relationship for all parties involved. The widowed parent isn't alone and has help around the house. The dual parents can enjoy the unmarried child's life while the 20-something child can avoid paying high rent.

The government sets a standard that makes us believe that these two situations of people living at home makes them "homeless." They are not; they have a roof over their head and a bed of their own—room and board. It's a fact that there are many among us who do live in cars or on the street, under bridges, or under trees in the parks.

As a caring society we offer them "homeless" shelters, free clothing, occasional work projects, low-cost food stamps, and publicly supported medical care. We have always offered them from early in their youth a constitutionally guaranteed free education.

We have showed them the dangers of using drugs and alcohol. Organizations such as Alcoholics Anonymous do a remarkably effective job for those who wish to rebuild their lives. Yet, even after they ignore all this, we still have it in our collective hearts to support community-based and faith-based soup kitchens. These are staffed by volunteers who feed these folks and provide warm shelters against the winter. Americans are famous for tackling these problems very well.

The borders do need some control. We are discussing what to do right now. We can't have the mess we have and keep ourselves safe from outside attack. Most of us welcome the new immigrants, however, as most of us are sons and daughters of immigrants, if we go back a few generations. Just waiting in line for your turn isn't too much to ask.

Our immigrant problem shows just how great this country really is. The Soviets built fences and posted guards to keep their folks *in!* We have people willing to take low-paying jobs and to start over at "the bottom," because it is still better for them here than "there."

The Middle East: Those folks have been fighting for centuries, much like the 800-year war between the Irish and the English, India vs. Pakistan, and African genocide, etc. We don't have the solution for any of it. We just need to be there to help them start talking, but we also need to realize that they have a different mind-set than Western thinking.

We have to convince the terrorist-training countries that supporting terror is unprofitable. Our military will continue to provide for a better world by making the ultimate sacrifice— Americans again to the rescue.

Schools are always under fire as everyone who ever attended school remembers how it was in the good ol' days. Much of the thinking is skewed today, as we test everyone, not just the kids who are the brightest. In "those days" the schools used to "lose" some of the kids around testing time. Americans decided we needed to accommodate everyone, so now the schools teach in dozens of different languages on the same campus.

We now teach special education students there instead of shipping them off somewhere else. Schools are held accountable for scores while parents keep the kids up late, don't check homework, and then blame the teachers. Nonetheless, scores on tests are still showing improvement in most segments of our society. We are addressing it and making it better.

Morality—most of us are good moral, ethical, honest folks who do what is right. The unfortunate thing is that we have a media that seems to cover only the negative in order to get attention. Most new stories sold to television or made into feature films are an exposé of the criminal mind and their activities. In contrast there are people who support great causes simply because it is the right thing to do.

There are great kids who behave and follow the teachings of their parents, and there are people who attend churches and temples and follow the teachings of their faith. Most of us follow the rules as we keep trying to learn and teach the lessons. This society knows the difference between right and wrong, and the vast majority of us generally does what is right.

Sorry, doom and gloomers, you're wrong...again!

22

Saved by My Imagination

by Ernie Weckbaugh

My whole life changed with a quiet knock on our front door. Our next-door neighbor decided to ask my mother if she would allow me to try out for a part in motion pictures. He was a director on contract with Warner Brothers Studios and, like many other people at that time in Hollywood, he was scouting around for little boys and girls to act in the *Little Rascals*, otherwise known as the *Our Gang Comedies*.

That was in the middle of the Great Depression of the 1930s, just before World War II. The chance to make extra money was always welcome, so her answer was an automatic "Yes!" At the age of five I didn't have much to say about it, although it further disrupted my childhood, already being torn apart by the wild war going on between my parents. Suddenly I had become the family pawn, another potential source of family finances, which was the main cause of my parents' conflict.

I had the opportunity to be employed in motion pictures up to the time I was ten. When Pearl Harbor was bombed, it effectively put an end to my career before it ever got started. My challenge during those four years in show business was to overcome boredom. I had to wait quietly on a sound stage for long hours every day, unable to play or make any noise. This would be a task for any six-year old. I never had a chance to make many friends, either on the sound stage or in elementary school. I was often taken out of school suddenly by my mother in the morning to report to a casting call, much to the envy of my classmates.

So I became a loner when I discovered I was able to draw and focused all my attention on art. I discovered writing stories was also fun, and my mother became my tutor, helping me to spell the words. I always brought a pad of paper everywhere I went, constantly drawing everything I saw or writing about it.

It seems that my whole childhood was a challenge to my imagination. It even happened when relatives would visit sunny California, escaping from the mid-western weather. They were always invited to stay by my father who played his role as the Hollywood Host for all it was worth. They would fill up every available bed in our tiny three-bedroom house. They shared our bedrooms, and often our beds. My parents were too polite to ever suggest they go to a hotel.

Without exception they all had ear-splitting snores that began when their heads hit their pillows after the food, drinks and conversation were finished and travel fatigue set in. I envied their ability to fall asleep immediately. The sound was deafening, so I decided to turn the noises into my own special sound effects.

I would pretend to be on a bombing raid over Europe, and I passed the hours heroically flying my four-engined bomber. My pillow was my parachute and their snoring provided the sound of the throbbing engines and the falling bombs. All the while I was using my imagination to maintain my sanity.

My parents divorced, and I was forced to testify at the hearings as they fought over my custody. I wasn't making much money at the time, but I was a potential "movie star." The idea terrified me. I found it hard to understand, especially what they wanted from me as a performer—to be an actor, singer, dancer...what?

After the war began, my mother and I moved to a nearby college campus where she received training as an aircraft engine inspector to do her part for the war effort. She felt a strong obligation since my older brother had just enlisted in the Navy and my sister married her high school sweetheart who became a fighter pilot. I never saw my father again.

My elementary school class was just a few blocks away from the college, but she told me I had to wait for several hours on the college campus after they let us out for my mother to finish her class in school.

That first day I went to her classroom, I was *stunned*. I saw the most amazing sight! On the lawn behind her building was a fighter plane, the most exciting aircraft of WWII. I had fallen in love with all of the beautifully sculptured aircraft they kept designing and manufacturing to fight our enemies.

There were no guards or fencing around it as there would most certainly be today. Anyone could walk up to it and climb all over it…and I did. It was a Lockheed P-38 Lightning, one of the most glamorous symbols of America's air superiority. Apparently I was the only one who knew it was there, and it quickly became my very own giant toy. Needless to say my imagination soared as I sat in it and maneuvered through dogfight fantasies by the hour, while waiting for my mother.

After my mother finished her course, we moved across the state to a large air base that repaired and modified airplanes. My mother had been trained for inspecting aircraft, and it seemed to me, wherever she was sent to work all over the state, it was one experience after another that unsettled me and overwhelmed my imagination.

One time on a school vacation day she was unable to find a babysitter for me. A good friend and fellow worker volunteered to spend a day of his vacation with me. He personally escorted me on a guided tour through every one of the countless WWII warplanes on the field. I must have acted like a star-struck kid.

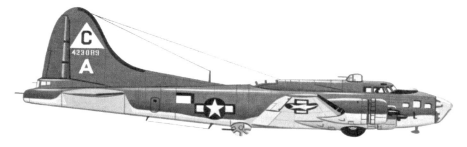

This truly was my "candy store." All of the model planes I had made with balsa wood suddenly became full-size. I was able to leave the sordid realities of my life: the tension of a bitter divorce, the constant traveling and relocating during wartime, attending nearly 10 different elementary schools, often changing in mid-semester. Again with my imagination I had another chance to escape the world into my own "reality."

A decade or so later when I was in the military during the Korean War, I remember going on practice combat alerts in the middle of the night. When we returned in the morning, we passed children playing war with their dad's helmets and jackets in the open fields of the base. My memory flashed back to those terrifying yet exciting days of my childhood. I saw again how imagination could become a constant companion, a friend who can carry us away to a safer place.

My own vivid imagination has saved me many times and always helped me to overcome challenges and find solutions to endless problems throughout my adult professional life. It has shown me how life doesn't have to be frightening, and how to do the things I love the most, with the people I love the most.

23

Reversing Difficulties

by Arthur T. Forrest, D.D.S.

I grew up as a child in the poorest of circumstances. I was from a single-parent home life, with only my mother, Ruby-Lee, who was a real life, lowly scrub maid who cleaned toilets and worked at two jobs. My mother also took in ironing to help support her family of three small children. Although mother only attended grade school to the fourth grade, she always encouraged me, telling me that I could be whatever I dreamed. I needed only to be willing to stay in school and work hard, not only with my hands but with my mind.

My dream of becoming a dentist started when I was only eight years old, even before *my* first visit to a dentist, when my mother had to have all of her remaining teeth removed to get full immediate dentures. I vowed right then and there, at eight years old, that I would become a dentist who "would not hurt people." That dream and promise carries on to the present day.

When I came to the USC School of Dentistry, I had two important role models early in my professional life. These were Dr. John Somerville and his wife, Dr. Vada Watson-Somerville. This remarkable man and wife dental team had been able to break down many barriers to help all those who followed.

The great USC School of Dentistry, which opened its doors for enrollment in 1897, had mirrored in many ways the conventions of the rest of the country. The ethnic diversity within USC has followed almost exactly the social consciousness of the nation. Among the over 9,000 doctorate (D.D.S.) graduates by the year 2000, fewer than 45 black dentists had graduated, with less than 10 involved in postgraduate specialty programs.

However, it was USC which had become the social leader in minority recruitment during a time when other private dental schools refused to admit black students. In the first half of the Twentieth Century, USC had voluntarily started a policy of admitting Blacks. Finally forced to change, due to the 1960 civil rights rulings of the United States Supreme Court, the remaining dental schools throughout the nation followed suit.

I first learned of the Somervilles when he arrived at USC. In the corridor next to the dean's office there was a portrait of Dr. John Somerville who had graduated in 1907. He was considered to be the first black person to graduate from the USC School of Dentistry. In spite of the many obstacles he had to face because of being black during that time, Dr. Somerville still obtained the highest grade-point average of his entire graduating class. He also scored and set a new record that same year for what were then the most points ever earned on the state board exams.

He later married the soon-to-be second black USC Dental School graduate, Dr. Vada Watson, who became the first black woman to receive a license to practice dentistry in the state of California. This couple, who built a successful practice together before the World War I, also built and owned the famous Dunbar Hotel in Los Angeles. Their guests and entertainers included Duke Ellington, Louis "Satchmo" Armstrong, Nat "King" Cole, Sammy Davis, Jr., Joe Louis, Jackie Robinson, and Jessie Owens. It became the center of the jazz culture in Los Angeles. The Drs. Somerville were also known to be among the original founders of the NAACP.

I proudly stepped into this environment of achievement. Dr. Somerville had established himself as a concerned man of action founding the USC Black Dental School Association. I ultimately became an enthusiastic member of the National Dental Association, the American Academy of Implant Dentistry, the American Academy of Cosmetic Dentistry, and the International Academy Congress of Oral Implantologists, among others. I was also elected to the be president of the USC Dental Alumni Association in the mid-1990s.

My dental training actually began in the U.S. Army as a dental assistant. I went on to become the base dental hygienist, and finally a dental laboratory technician at Ft. Riley, Kansas. This was at the height of the Vietnam War of 1966-69.

Like many other vets, I attended college at night on the G.I. Bill and was accepted to the USC School of Dentistry in 1974, graduating in 1978. At USC, due to financial hardships, I had to travel to dental school from Pomona on the bus, 101 miles round trip daily, requiring six transfers. I traveled four hours each day by bus. My classmates must have known I was dedicated.

I always seem to have a knack for reversing difficult situations. Very soon after I entered dental school, I used my dental experience and knowledge of metal castings and gold working to start what eventually became a successful jewelry manufacturing and retail sales business. We succeeded in placing my creations into the major malls under the appropriate name "Black Forrest Jewelry." Eventually it grew into a chain of 17 stores known as Earthcraft.

By my junior year, two years later, I no longer needed the bus. Still in dental school I was able to purchase a brand new Porsche 944 for my wife and a new Cadillac Seville for myself.

Our home in Chino Hills has really become our dream "castle." Toni and I have four children: Vanessa (left), Toni (middle), Kaniesha (right), Arthur II and Aiesha (in Art's lap).

Years later we contracted and helped construct a 7,000-square-foot home in Chino Hills, which we have affectionately named "Graystone Castle." This was followed by the construction of a 2,000 square foot dental office also in Chino. We moved there from Pomona where we lived and, by then, I had practiced for 17 years.

My son, Arthur Forrest II, says, "I want to be a USC dentist, just like my Dad." After all of my ambitious and creative activities over the years, I will be soon be in need of some help with my very busy practice and other enterprises.

For both my home and office, I did my own electrical, plumbing, security, designing, painting and finished carpentry. I even recruited my beautiful wife Toni to stain all the doors, cabinetry, and woodwork.

I remember my mother's admonition about hard work. Over the years I have had so many great inspirations, beginning with her, and then Drs. Somerville and Watson.

I don't believe success comes any other way.

24

See the Stars

by Gayleen Williams

You can think yourself happy. "Happiness is really an attitude. We either make ourselves miserable, or happy and strong. The amount of work is the same," said Francesca Reigler. Perspective determines all of our beliefs, and our beliefs in turn, determine our attitude. One definition of attitude is "a feeling or emotion toward a fact or state." Our thought determines feeling. And our feeling determines our action. Perspective is absolutely vital to our happiness. People who have overcome much in their life understand this.

Life is not the way it's supposed to be, it's the way it is.

Famed author and speaker Virginia Satir said, "The way you cope with life is what makes the difference." She also said, "I think if I have one message, one thing before I die that most of the world should know, it would be that the event does not determine how to respond to the event. That is a purely personal matter. The way in which we respond will direct and influence the event more than the event itself."

It's all in our perception. Whether we see everything from a negative perspective or a positive perspective determines our life experiences. Lee Piper said, "The mind cannot be trusted. We can think ourselves into anything."

Earl Nightingale expressed, "A great attitude does much more than turn on the lights in our world; it seems to magically connect us to all sorts of serendipitous opportunities that were somehow absent before the change." ivillage.com shared, "Think happiness happens by luck or chance? Not so! The truth is that you can cultivate a happy and positive outlook on life – no fairy godmother required."

We may not be responsible for the action; however, we are responsible for our reaction to the action. It's not a question of good or bad things happening to us. It's how we interpret what happens to us. We are in charge of our attitudes.

Here's a real life example: For many years on special occasions my mother would have us all gather several hours before dinner. She, of course, just wanted to have us with her longer. However people got quite hungry and therefore irritable due to their blood sugar dropping from lack of food. We'd sit down to eat and everyone would be grouchy and complaining. I would always get an upset stomach and rush to the bathroom.

One evening we sat down to dinner and as usual the bickering began. I was calmly eating my food – and enjoying it, I might add. I deliberately looked up from my food, made eye contact with each of my three brothers and said, "Wow! This food is so delicious. The rest of you should choose to be enjoying it, too." And, I went back to enjoying my dinner.

An unusual silence came over the room. Everyone else began eating, too! I later explained to my mother what had occurred. She began to prepare snacks to enjoy before the meal, which helped control irritability from low blood sugar. I choose to no longer buy into the chaos. What do you want to change?

There are a number of maxims that illustrate perspective.

"Two men looked through prison bars; one saw mud, the other saw stars." Happiness isn't having what we want; it's wanting what we have. When one door of happiness closes, another opens, but often we look so long at the closed door that we don't see the one that has been opened for us.

Attitude is more important than facts. It is more important than our past, more important than how much money we have, more important than how much education we have, and even more important than circumstances. It is more important than what other people think, say, or do and more important than how beautiful or handsome we are, and more important than our talents or skills. It is my opinion that our attitude determines almost everything; it is one of the most important factors in our happiness.

Use the words "creative challenge."

Don't use the word "problem." People also refer to "unexpected outcomes" or "pending solutions." You may say this is just semantics. However, that computer we call a brain responds much better to positive input. No meaningful goal is without obstacles. View these "obstacles" as "challenges" that are part of the journey to success and see them favorably.

Our attitude determines our happiness. No matter what the circumstances, we can remain hopeful if we choose. People who are hopeful are optimistic. They believe that bad things are temporary and changeable. Optimists are less vulnerable to depression, achieve more, and have better health.

Erich Fromm stated that, "Psychologically speaking, destructiveness is the alternative to hope." His theory is that violence is a result of hopelessness.

How we handle stress depends upon our attitude and how it handles us.

Men and women suffering from depression have a 70 percent greater risk of a heart attack and a 60 percent higher risk of dying, according to a Duke University study. Another study conducted by the University of Texas concluded that people with an upbeat view of life were less likely than pessimists to show signs of frailty. Scientists have discovered that worry, negativity, and stress can cause our brains to produce chemicals that can harm our bodies. Stress also allows more free radicals to attack our systems. Free radicals speed up our aging process and increase our chances of disease.

The philosopher William James said, "The greatest discovery of my generation is that a human being can alter his life by altering his attitude." Knowing we always have options and choices, we can choose new attitudes and change our life. My mother said it incredibly well: "We give power to people and circumstances, when actually the power is in our own mind!"

Steve Allen said, "One of the nice things about problems is that a good many of them do not exist except in our imaginations." Eleanor Roosevelt also stated, "No one can make you feel inferior without your consent."

Martin Seligman shared, "Depression is a result of a belief in one's own helplessness." Mildred Barthel said, "Happiness is a conscious choice, not an automatic response."

Events and circumstances have power over us only if we allow them to. We choose to stay angry or sad. We can change our attitude. We may not be able to change the circumstance but we can change our attitude about it. It's not our problems that get us down – it's how we view them. It's our decision that we allow them into our life. We have no control over other people; however we do control the effect their attitudes or opinions have on us. We have control over our perspective.

Remember you have choices and options and you have power. If we "choose" something, we are in control. If we let things happen to us, we are not in control. Actually we are always making choices. Even not choosing is a choice.

We "choose" to go to work.

We believe we "have" to go to work. So, instead we can say, "I *'want'* to go to work." The choice of words may seem trivial, but it reflects our attitude. It's more effective and satisfying to say we "choose to."

Absolutely no one shares our perception or views life exactly as we do. We see the world uniquely. It's our choice how we see life. So, how do you see life? Do you see a cloud or do you see the blue sky behind it? Do we see the rain or do we see the chance for things to grow? Do we see a windy day or do we see a chance to fly a kite? Do we see obstacles or opportunities? Is the glass half-full or half-empty? The contents of the glass don't change; however our attitude can. When I say, "With my luck...," it's a negative thought. I've learned instead to attach a positive expectancy to it.

Most people tend to focus on the negative aspects of an event instead of the positives. Ask yourself "What is the worst thing that can happen? ... And, what's the worst thing about that? ... And, what's the worst thing about that?" This usually shrinks the matter from a mountain to a molehill in your mind. Another approach to this is to ask, "What is the truth about this situation? ... What can I do to make it better?" It's up to us how we see things and how we respond.

Shift your perception by taking a step back. By distancing yourselves things become less important. Think of the human mind as a magnifying glass. It exaggerates things. Whatever you think the challenge is, it's probably not as bad as you think. Develop a positive attitude by reframing your perspective.

Often we go through life living for tomorrow, living for some future event or set of circumstances. We convince ourselves that things will be better when this, that, or the other thing happens.

Marshall Goldsmith said it well, "The great Western disease is, 'I'll be happy when. When I get the money. When I get a BMW. When I get that job.' Well, the reality is, you will *never* get to 'when.' The only way to find happiness is to understand that happiness is not out there. It's in here. Happiness is not next week. It's now." Let's not postpone our happiness. There's no better time than now to be happy. You will always have creative challenges of one kind or another in your life. Why not just accept this and decide to be happy anyway?

The simple truth is: we get just exactly what we expect!

My family was poor, so I should not have expected that I could go to college. However, my mother always told me that I would go to college. So I had an expectation of my future that included college. I expected to go to college and to college I went. With the "belief" that I was going to college, I studied diligently and applied myself to college prep courses, earning scholarship funds, a grant, and student loans. It never occurred to me that I might not be able to go to college. Thanks Mom.

Aristotle expressed, "What you expect, that you shall find." We get what we feel we deserve. Dr. Robert Anthony said, "Your expectations of today will be your life of tomorrow." He also expressed, "Expectations control your life, so it is imperative that you control your expectations. If you expect the best, the best you shall have. But if you expect the worst to happen, be assured that it will. By permitting your life to be dominated by negative thought patterns, you form the habit of expecting negative results. Studies show that 90 percent of people have negative expectations."

These negative expectations are also referred to as limiting beliefs. So why don't people just change their beliefs? They simply don't recognize that the beliefs they currently hold are limiting and preventing them from getting what they want in life. They also may not be allowing enough time for change. If you have areas in your life that need improvement, you probably have made a limiting decision. It is estimated that 90 percent of us have limiting beliefs, usually made when we were children. Once you identify a decision, you can choose to change it and have what you really want in life! A Jewish king once said something like this, "Don't ever wish yourself anything bad."

I once wrote a boyfriend a poem about his being a free bird and that I was not trying to catch him but just wanted to enjoy the flight with him. He told me that every time he thought about leaving I let him go and he had no reason to leave. Later I became fearful of losing him – and so I did. In fact, I lost him within two weeks of fearing losing him. Ah, the power of expectation.

Expectation focuses on the future.

Use expectation positively. An expectation of bad things is an act of fear. Fear is perceived; fear is an attitude. Since we can change our attitude, we can change our fear. It is my firm belief that the main thing, if not the only thing that truly limits us in life, is FEAR. Without fear, we experience peace and happiness. Things are not always as they seem. We often perceive a situation as negative when it is not. We allow current situations to cloud our beliefs.

Avoid mistaken certainties.

Ponder that idea a minute. This phrase comes from one of my favorite authors, Robert Anthony. Another author, Rhonda Britten, said, "Whether you know it or not, fear has developed your likes and dislikes, picked your friends, and raised your children." Fear can affect every aspect of our lives. So learn to release fear and get on with your life and being happy.

Life is not just a series of great events for us to remember or for us to plan. Life is made up of innumerable small events that unfold minute-by-minute, hour-by-hour, and day-by-day. Mark Twain said, "Dance like nobody's watching; love like you've never been hurt. Sing like nobody's listening; live like it's heaven on earth."

Count your blessings and keep your attitude positive. Live with positive expectancy as Wayne Dyer does. He said, "I am realistic—I expect miracles."

I have had so many miracles in my life the last couple of years that I now expect them, and so they keep showing up. Thank you, God! One of my miracles was winning Tom Antion's $5,000 Internet Marketing weekend workshop. I also got a free ticket worth $497 to an empowerment summit. Just lucky, you may say. There have been too many things to just call them luck!

25

Action Is the Key

by Gayleen Williams

Happy people are action oriented. They know taking action is key in getting what they want in life. I am convinced that action is the most significant thing you can do to empower yourself. Action is truly the catalyst. You can read about, learn about, talk about, philosophize about, and desire to change things. However, without action, nothing happens, *ABSOLUTELY NOTHING.*

Joe Sabah says, "You do not have to be great to start, but you have to start to be great."

According to Barbara Sher, "Success does not depend on how you feel. Human moods have remarkably little to do with effective action."

Action is Essential.

Pablo Picasso is quoted as saying, "Action is the foundational key to all success. Action is absolutely critical. You must take action for anything to happen or change."

H. J. Brown, Jr. said poetically, "Opportunity dances with those already on the dance floor."

In *Celebrate Your Self,* Dorothy Corkville Briggs said, "Awareness, courage and decision need to be coupled with action. Recipes in books don't bake cookies. You do—through action. Blueprints on paper don't build bridges. People hard at work do. Here are the tools you need. But only you can decide to use them, to practice them daily."

Maya Angelou expressed, "Nothing will work unless you do." Nolan Bushnell also shared, "Everyone who has ever taken a shower has had an idea. It's the person who gets out of the shower, dries off, and does something about it who makes a difference."

Action is such a positive thing. Action is movement. Action is motion. Action is what drives us forward. Action energizes us. Action mobilizes us. Action is healthy; it has been proven that positive chemicals called endorphins are created in our bodies when we take action.

Dr. Norman Vincent Peale said, "Action is the restorer and builder of confidence. Inaction is not only the result, but the cause of fear. Perhaps the action you take will be successful; perhaps different action or adjustments will have to follow. But any action is better than no action at all." Don't view failure negatively—just as the adjustments necessary for success.

No matter what your challenges are, when you make the conscious decision to take action you turn the tide of life in your favor. Opportunities will present themselves in most unusual ways. You will find yourself involved in new and interesting endeavors. Action has a way of increasing opportunity.

Benjamin Disraeli said, "Action does not always bring happiness, but there is no happiness without action." I believe action cures fear. Life really is as simple as—if something in your life doesn't work, change it. Move away from it or accept it! If you don't like something, then change it or accept it.

The best way to escape a problem is to solve it. A friend named Linda once said, "A problem does not present itself without an answer somewhere in it."

The very successful Lee Iacocca expressed, "Apply yourself. Get all the education you can, but then, by God, do something. Don't just stand there, make it happen."

Margot Fonteyn, the legendary ballerina, when asked how she survived her many challenges in life answered, "I have no idea. I was performing; I simply got out there and danced. And I live that way too. I don't analyze. I just get on with it."

I "Hope" I Can.

When we use the words "hope" and "try" we simply limit ourselves. It's almost an excuse in advance not to take action Having "tried" once or twice, it becomes an excuse to give up, and "hoping" can take the place of any real effort on our part. We don't want to stop "trying" and we certainly don't want to give up "hope." We just need to put the words into proper perspective. "Hope" is a friend to all, especially to the happiness action tool of courage. As we're about to jump into the "unknown" where all those imaginary monsters dwell, "hope" stands beside us and reminds us that here is where all our potential good resides.

You either hit the ball or you don't hit the ball. You do or you don't. You really can't "try" to do something. Why set yourself up for disappointment. Be positive in taking action. See yourself as having accomplished whatever it is you want. Practice it in your mind. It has been proven that when we practice in our mind, we make fewer mistakes.

Robert Anthony, one of my favorite authors and speakers, says that, "Excuses are a lack of faith in our own power. If you simply wish and hope for something to happen, you are not utilizing the force of action. James Russell Lowell put it this way, "All the sentiments in the world weigh less than one lovely action!"

Just stop and think before using the words "hope" or "try." They may imply possible failure. Use the statements, "I will" or "I intend" or "I plan" to show probable accomplishment. Check your "intentions." They're based in integrity and they're full of heart. Then just *do it.*

Now understand that I recognize the positive interpretations of these words. "Try" is the first step after the decision "to do" and that "hope" is a messenger that the dreams we have are not just dreams but signs of our unlimited possibilities.

Here are a few more words of caution. Please don't take action just to take action. Think before you jump. Don't be busy just to be busy! Spend your energy on productive action. The power of thought behind the action is even more significant than the action itself. Don't become preoccupied with mindless "doing." Have purpose and be mindful of your underlying intention.

Action is taken one step at a time. In *The Magic of Thinking Big*, David J. Swartz said, "The person determined to achieve maximum success learns the principle that progress is made a step at a time. A house is built a brick at a time. Football games are won a play at a time. A store grows bigger one new customer at a time. Every big accomplishment is a series of little accomplishments."

Lao Tzu said, "The journey of a thousand miles begins with a single step." Al Bernstein shared, "Sometimes the fool who rushes in gets the job done." Let's face it: If you don't start, it's certain you won't finish. William Blake told us, "Execution is the chariot of genius." Mark Twain expressed, "The secret of getting ahead is getting started. The secret of getting started is breaking your complex overwhelming tasks into small manageable tasks, and then starting on the first one." Will Rogers said, "Even if you're on the right track, you'll get run over just sitting there."

Nike Ads Encourage Us to JUST DO IT!

We're all guilty of procrastination at one time or another. We then waste even *more* time criticizing ourselves for procrastinating! Why do we procrastinate? To avoid something we don't want to do or because we have a need for perfection. Instead of just doing something to the best of our ability now, we put it off until we have more information on how to do it right, have better tools, or until someone can help us with it. Often if we just go ahead and do it with what's at hand it will turn out better than we expected. Is what you are avoiding really a priority in your life? What will happen if you don't do this now? Will you still need to do it later? If not, maybe it really isn't important to do it at all. Maybe you can "choose" to just let it go. If you decide it is necessary, the next question is how important is this? If it is important, then do it and get it over with. The pay off is you feel good about yourself. You aren't wasting valuable time on that nagging thought that something isn't done.

Here's a simple idea for overcoming procrastination from time-management experts. Just commit to making an effort toward a project for ten minutes only. When your ten-minutes is up you may be in the mood and motivated enough to continue.

Starting with a small action, we can often accomplish major feats. Take that first step. Somehow just getting started makes the whole project seem more achievable.

We take action in the present, in the *NOW!* My mother said it quite profoundly, "We are all so busy becoming, when all we need to do is be."

An unknown author said, "Remember yesterday, dream about tomorrow — but live today!" But my very favorite quote of all time is by Johann Wolfgang von Goethe:

> *"What you can do or dream you can, begin it;*
> *boldness has genius, power and magic in it."*

You've heard the expression, "After all is said and done, much is said and little is done." If you don't start, it's certain you won't arrive. So, go take action! Go build your happiest life!

26

Sammy Davis, Jr.
A Study in Beating the Odds

by Arthur Silber, Jr.

One thing that life continually teaches us is that achieving anything worthwhile will probably involve the following immutable factors: 1) It will take talent, focus, untold hours of sacrifice and hard work, 2) it will bring forth unknowable and innumerable road blocks from elements of society and the laws of nature, 3) the better you are and the higher you rise will often bring out the worst in those who have neither the talent nor the success, 4) and the same people who tried to undermine your success will praise you when you are gone.

The life of Sammy Davis, Jr., whose multi-faceted talent was a wonder to behold, is an example of all these rules of human existence. Born in the proverbial trunk, he was raised on the vaudeville stages of the 1930s and '40s, with no formal education. He learned his craft by standing in the wings of the stage and watching all the legends of the time, like Bill (Bojangles) Robinson who taught Sammy all his dance steps. He learned the many aspects of life experienced by the individuals around him. His father, Sammy Davis, Sr. and uncle, Will Mastin, who ran the Will Mastin Trio, saw to it that the young boy was shielded from racism by their being booked only into cities that were considered safe for them to perform.

During World War II Sammy was drafted into the Army and got an awakening to racism in some very nasty ways. Sammy commented about the experience. "Overnight the world looked different. It wasn't one color anymore. I could see the protection I'd gotten all my life from my father and Will," he would later say. "I appreciated their loving hope that I'd never need to know about prejudice and hate, but they were wrong. It was as if I'd walked through a swinging door for 18 years, a door which they had always secretly held open—but then it swung back and hit me in the face."

As Sammy began to come into his own as a solo star in the late 1940s and early '50s, it became clear to everyone that his overwhelming talent was going to take him to great heights. My father had managed the Will Mastin Trio for many years until his dad's death in 1954. I started to get close to Sammy during a trip to Hawaii in 1949. This fateful trip began a brotherhood between Sammy and myself that lasted the better part of 23 years, until he passed in 1990. We become partners in business and the closest of confidants as Sammy made the transition from member of a trio to an internationally renowned and beloved performer. I chronicled these years in my book, *Sammy Davis, Jr.: Me and My Shadow.*

But to get to that place in history, Sammy had to battle every step of the way. In all of Sammy's struggles I believe he deserves more recognition in the fight for civil rights. When I hear discussions about pioneers who broke down color barriers, seldom is the name of Sammy Davis, Jr. spoken of at all. During the 1950s we had to avoid certain cities for fear of retribution due to his skin color. The fact that I was white and Jewish caused me to share with him some quite painful experiences and emotions when he would say, "Arthur, all I really want is to be equal."

Before the major gains were made during the Civil Rights movement of the 1960s, Sammy had been breaking down racial barriers all over the country during the '50s for those who would follow. For example, he and every performer of color who performed in Las Vegas hotels were not permitted to stay at the hotel, eat in the restaurants, or gamble in the casinos. They all had to leave through the back doors by the garbage bins.

After years of suffering quietly under these pernicious conditions, Sammy got fed up and thus began the infighting with management, the mob, and the powers behind the scenes. It didn't happen easily and didn't happen overnight, but the barriers would be broken down—sometimes facing the threat of death. But

Sammy pushed down those barriers one at a time, and the world is better off because of it.

In another incident, Sammy, with a bit of help from his good friend Frank Sinatra, was able to break the color barrier at the famous Copacabana Club in New York City. When Sinatra performed at the club, whose owner had a particular dislike for blacks, Sammy was allowed in to watch Frank do his act, but he was forced to sit at the back of the bar in the shadows. After this went on for a while, the proprietor complained to Sinatra about having to allow Sammy into the club.

Having had enough of the grousing, Sinatra told him in no uncertain terms, "If you want to book the best, then you are going to have to let Sammy Davis, Jr., perform here. If you don't book Sammy, you can forget about me ever performing here again." Sammy was booked into the Copacabana and proceeded to break house records while also bringing the first black patrons into the club. Thus another barrier of hatred was broken down by this diminutive yet powerful force of nature.

But as time went on, he joined Martin Luther King, Jr., in his drive for racial equality and fought for the rights of all people of color. Sammy did all this while living through two knee replacements and a new hip. As he still strived to entertain the world, he fought the good fight and in the process became a credit to his country and to people of all creeds and colors.

I guess the most horrific single thing that happened to Sammy in his younger life took place in the morning of a cold and crisp day in November 1954. While driving down a two-lane highway in San Bernardino on his way to record the title song for a movie. Sammy saw that the road in front of him was completely blocked with cars which forced his car to swerve off the road and run into a solid concrete wall. When he was rescued, they found his left eye had come out of its socket and was lying on his cheek. This resulting in his loss of sight, necessitating an artificial eye. Also his nose was broken and his knee cap was cracked.

While lying in a hospital bed, he didn't know for three days if he would ever see again through the remaining eye, as the nerves of the eyes are interconnected. But God prevailed and gave him back the one good eye. One would think that was a blessing, and in fact it was; but this created major problems for Sammy, as he did not know if he would ever be able to dance again, because of the affect this would have on his balance.

Given that to overcome, and not being able to see anything from the left side of his nose, created another problem. He wasn't sure if he would be able to see where the stage ended, which was the side where his Uncle Will was always dancing. Would he bump into him or possibly fall off the stage? But with the help of all of us, his family and his conductor, Sammy was able to overcome this one great obstacle. No one ever knew what it took for him to achieve this. Just another door to push his way through. I can only thank God I was not in his car that day.

When I reflect on Sammy Davis, Jr.'s life and my time with him, words that describe him such as versatile, dynamic, kinetic and exciting swirl through my mind's eye. A sensitive man with towering talent and a love of performing, Sammy could do it all: sing, dance, play multiple instruments and act with a flair for comedy as well as a feel for drama. My sincere hope is that Sammy will be remembered for his God-given talent and his courage in the face of adversity. I know that would also be his wish as well.

To put it simply, Sammy Davis, Jr., was one of a kind.

27

Joaquin's Bike Accident

by Yolanda Nava

As I reflect on some of life's larger tragedies, I find they often provide opportunities to test my faith and gain in gratitude. I have meant for some years to write about the terrible bicycle accident that sent my 10-year old son to the hospital for brain surgery, because it turned out to be one of the most uplifting times of my life.

The morning of the accident, Joaquin asked if he could ride his bike to school. Our hilly South Pasadena neighborhood has narrow streets with dangerous curves that gave me pause, but it was a beautiful sunny day, and I agreed that he could not live in fear. "Yes, you may," I said, but added, "Just ride around the school yard once you get there. Do *not* stay on the main street."

Unfortunately, boys will be boys, and my warning was not heeded. Shortly after Joaquin left for school I received a call from the school nurse. "Joaquin has had a bicycle accident in front of the school," she reported. "He seems okay; he's just a bit shaken up, but I think you should keep him home for the day."

My husband Art was fortunately still at home and left to pick up our son. I stayed behind with our four-year-old daughter Danielle. When Joaquin arrived at home and described the accident I shuddered, and immediately thanked God. He had been riding up and down the street in front of the elementary school at the base of the canyon with another school chum. The boys were both going downhill chasing after a ball riding parallel to the curb on their bicycles when Joaquin's tire hit the curb and threw him over the handlebars to the ground. Thankfully he landed on a grassy area and not the sidewalk, but he landed on his head. He wasn't wearing a helmet. There were no signs of trauma, but I had heard about an injury similar to his that had no immediate symptoms.

As Joaquin had landed on the right side of his head near his eye, I took him to an eye doctor that morning. He found nothing wrong with his eyes but recommended getting an X-ray "just in case." My son seemed fine and in good spirits for the rest of the day.

The following morning everything had changed. His speech was slurred and incomprehensible: he was feeling low in energy. It was obvious he had sustained a concussion. His father immediately took him to a doctor friend, noted neurologist Edward Zapanta, while I prepared to take Danielle to pre-school. I consciously tried to alleviate my fears, and realized we needed some metaphysical help.

I looked at the clock. It was 8:55 a.m. I knew Dr. Bill Hornaday, the minister of the Founder's Church of Religious Science did prayers for the congregation each morning at 9 a.m. I dialed his office and Carol Hatch, his chief of staff answered in her customary cheery voice, and after I told her why we needed their prayers, she immediately handed the telephone to "Dr. Bill."

In a calm voice, I described the situation. I will never forget my minister's initial response: "Now we know that Joaquin is just perfect," and he went on to say other words to affirm my son's wholeness. Dr. Hornaday was a wonderful metaphysician, minister and speaker. His loving and deep, clear voice conveyed a spirit of encouragement, hope and healing that sustained me for the entire week Joaquin was in the critical care unit of Children's Hospital.

After several hairline fractures were discovered by the CAT scan ordered by the neurologist, I thought "hairline" meant Joaquin might be able to forego surgery. "No, no," Art told me from the telephone at Dr. Zapanta's office. "He needs surgery to repair the fractures, and Dr. Zapanta has arranged for him to be admitted. Children's Hospital have some of the best children's neurosurgeons."

When we arrived at the hospital, Dr. Miles Little, the neurosurgeon on duty, had been alerted and was expecting us. He was tall and good-looking, with a hint of a southern accent and a gentle and loving manner as he examined Joaquin. After the examination, Dr. Little informed us that he would not be able to perform the needed surgery for a few days. There were only two surgeons on duty working 16-18 hours a day, and there were several emergency cases ahead of us.

The delay turned out to be a blessing. Joaquin's head had

swollen up to the point where his face was round and flat like a plate, resembling that of a four-hundred pound Sumo wrestler. By the time the surgery took place, some of the swelling had subsided. The lessening of the urgency of the situation allowed me to deeply immerse myself in a wonderful metaphysical book, *The Edinburgh Lectures* by Thomas Troward.

It is difficult to describe my state of mind that week. I felt full of inspiration (a word that means literally to take in *spirit*), clear and buoyant. I didn't want to tell anyone about the accident to avoid others' negative thoughts of fear and concern. I knew Art's parents would be worried about their first grandson, and my mother-in-law had a tendency to fret. But I didn't want any negativity. I told Art to talk to his parents. "If your mother is going to come in here saying, 'Oh, poor Joaquin,' and be full of apprehension and anxiety, I'd rather she stay away."

I was adamant. The only person I told about the accident was my dear friend Roseanne Dimbeck, a doctor of chiropractic, who happened to call just as we were leaving for the hospital. She turned out to be a Godsend.

I was so completely imbued with the spirit of wholeness that when Dr. Little ticked off the things that could go wrong as a result of the surgery, required under malpractice laws, I denied each negative suggestion and said, "I know that my son is perfect and that God is working through your hands." His reaction was one of surprise, but then he gave me a long, gentle look of comprehension I will never forget.

Art and I also experienced the desire to support other parents in the hospital rather than focus on our own son. The hospital critical care unit was full. Several children diagnosed with terminal illnesses like leukemia were also staying in a nearby ward. Art was a politician who almost became a pediatrician, and was always willing to help others. So we spent time with the children and their Spanish-speaking parents, to give them encouragement and words of hope.

Somehow the word of Joaquin's hospitalization spread from coast to coast. Art began to receive telephone calls of support. Joaquin's room began to fill up with gifts. One of his favorite admirers, Assemblyman Curtis Tucker, sent an enormous box of Star Wars toys. Of course, the gifts made the hospital experience a positive one for a young boy.

Roseanne came to the hospital and provided tremendous emotional and physical support. She massaged Joaquin's body and we worked his little legs back and forth as if he were riding his bicycle or pedaling a boat, and to keep him from being bored, singing "Row, row, row your boat," as we did so. He giggled with delight. Strangely, on another occasion, Joaquin asked Roseanne, who is half Japanese (but *how* did he know that?), if she knew any Japanese songs? She began to croon to him softly in a language I did not understand. His face beamed with joy.

The surgery was more complicated than anticipated and took an unexpected five hours, rather than two. Art and I went out for dinner and a movie. After the surgery, Dr. Little explained the severity of the operation. "We had to saw open Joaquin's head from ear to ear, and take bone fragments from behind his head to help fill the indentation caused by the blow to his forehead. Fortunately the *dura* (the outer covering of the brain) was not torn as a result of the fracture." Dr. Little described how the ophthalmologist also had to peel his face forward and pop Joaquin's eyes out of his skull in order for the plastic surgeon to reconstruct the area behind his nose. Half of his sinuses had been crushed. The doctors then placed his eyes back in place and wired and stapled his skull back together.

"Your son may have some temporary sight problems for a few weeks until things have settled down," the doctor advised. When we saw our son in the recovery room, he was in good spirits, and I knew our prayers were answered.

Within days Joaquin was bathing at home and tormenting his sister by exposing his ear-to-ear scar. He had lost weight and was very skinny. He looked a bit frightening, so little Danielle asked him to cover his head with a shower cap when the bandages were removed. Only two weeks later Joaquin was playing ball at school. He has been in perfect health ever since.

The son of a friend's neighbor in Beverly Hills, who had a similar bicycle accident that same week, was not so fortunate. He died from his injuries. Hearing this, I realized how fortunate we were. I again express my gratitude for the life and health of Joaquin, and for the health of our entire family. I have repeated that gratitude over and over since that time, and I continue to revel in the power of prayer.

What is it that allows healing for some and not others? I wonder. I can't believe that God, who is all goodness and knowing, rewards some and punishes others. Could it be the certainty with which we know that perfection and health is ours—if only we acknowledge and accept this truth.

I only know that the week we spent at Children's Hospital after Joaquin's accident was an extraordinary week in my life— one filled with inspiration, certainty, hope and healing. It was a miraculous time. Even the hospital president, Jane Hurd, to this day, refers to Joaquin as "our miracle child."

28

The Perfect Day

by Eva Rosenberg

Airplanes have always fascinated me, even as a toddler. When I was only two, anytime an airplane passed overhead, I was compelled to stop and stare, marveling at how that big, beautiful metal creature could stay up in the sky without dropping.

At age three, the first time I ever saw an airplane up close, I was astonished. We were in an Austrian airport and this DC-6 rolled to a stop before our gate. It had wheels! It had never occurred to me that an airplane would have wheels. But, thinking it over, I thought it was right and fitting for it to have wheels. What a special treat it was to get to fly in it. Back then, only the very wealthy could afford to fly—and we were simply destitute Jewish refugees. But somehow, someone, perhaps it was the Hebrew Immigration Aid Society (HIAS) who funded our tickets.

What an experience! The seats faced each other, with a removable table in between. We could eat on it, play cards, tell stories to each other…or have my daddy tell me fairy tales to put me to sleep. When the tabletop was removed, you could stretch out and sleep. You could look down and see the cities, farms and tiny people below.

Flighty experiences have followed me throughout my life. Somehow, I managed to end up dating men who flew. One man and one day are the most memorable of all—my long distance romance.

Chris was vice president of an international company and traveled worldwide. Since his corporation was doing well, he had the company fund the cost of his flying lessons, and actually did use those skills to host executives from around the world. And me.

Since we lived so far apart, and we were both busy, we didn't get to see each other very often. But those times were memorable. One evening, Chris called and asked, "What are you doing tomorrow?" Flushed with excitement, I replied that I could clear my day, but not my dinner plans for the evening. He said, "Fine. Grab a plane and come on up. I promise you'll be home in time for your dinner party."

The next morning, I practically floated to John Wayne Airport and hopped on an Air Cal flight to the Bay Area. The window seat was available. So I had a window seat and a row to myself. Chris greeted me passionately. Then escorted me to his classy chassis, his pet Mercedes. We chattered excitedly, catching up during the surprisingly brief trip to our next destination—another airport. Chris had reserved a little four-seater Bonanza for our day.

He gave me a panoramic aerial tour of the whole Bay Area, flying over part of Napa and the vineyards, and out over the Golden Gate Bridge and over the Lawrence Livermore Labs where he told me about the cyclotron. For the longest time we just flew and floated freely, like the birds. Just when I was getting lost in the fantasy, he reached for his microphone and checked in with a control tower. He arranged for clearance to land and for ground transportation.

Seconds later, we were on a landing strip in the middle of nowhere. It led to a small tarmac area where three other private planes were parked. Suddenly, a train whistle shrilled...and along the tracks next to the planes came the smallest, cutest train. Even though it was toy-sized, it did carry passengers—and we were invited. A-a-a-a-ll abo-o-o-o-ard!

We'd landed at the Nut Tree Airport in Vacaville, CA. The Nut Tree Railroad was escorting us to the landmark Nut Tree Restaurant. What a magical little place.

The restaurant served such wonderful food that they were even called upon to cater for royalty. There was a toy factory, a gift shop, fresh fruits, souvenirs, a bakery and a candy kitchen.

Apparently, Edwin "Bunny" Power's little family oasis along US Interstate 80, leading from Sacramento and the Bay Area to Lake Tahoe, has been here since 1921, long before Disneyland was even conceived. Over 50 years later, even in the middle of the week, it was filled with lots of happy people, especially children, racing about excitedly. It's the kind of place you simply couldn't imagine anyone frowning.

We were happy, too, and filled with lots of energy. So we walked around, my feet barely touching the ground, exploring the treasures the Nut Tree had to offer and sampling the goodies. The day was hot—well over 90 degrees. The sun beat down on us. Our faces were starting to turn pink. Uh-oh, we suddenly realized that we were dehydrated and on the verge of sunstroke. We needed to find a place to cool down—fast.

Looking up, we suddenly saw a place with a fairy tale name. While I can't remember it now, at the time there was something so apt about the name that it made us laugh. It seemed to appear just because we needed it.

Checking in, we frolicked under the cooling spray from a mist generator. Finally, cooled off and refreshed, we ran to catch the Nut Tree Railroad heading back to Chris's Bonanza.

Flying back to catch my flight, we were quieter. Only, our laughter kept bubbling over. We couldn't seem to repress our delicious mood.

Chris kept his word, reluctantly. He put me back on Air Cal and got me back to my dinner party in Newport Beach in plenty of time. My friends never knew why I couldn't stop smiling all night. Now the secret is out.

It was one of the best days ever—totally spontaneous, magic and completely fulfilling.

Today, decades later, Chris and I are happily and contentedly married to others. My husband and I were the only non-family members at Chris's intimate wedding.

That perfect day lives on. Memories are all that's left of this luscious day. The Bonanza has gone to the little airplane graveyard in the sky. So has Air Cal, the Nut Tree Restaurant, the railroad, the toy factory, the bakery, and the shops...all were leveled by "progress."

Though, with all the people who keep it alive on the Internet and in family albums, postcard collections and stories, and the memories, there is talk of bringing it back—well, at least the Nut Tree railroad and restaurant, and the family atmosphere.

So, if you ever see me smiling for no apparent reason, you'll know I am reliving this memory—this perfect day.

Numbers into Words

5338	bees	53705514	his soles
39138	beige	378804	hobble
5938	begs	50804	hobos
57738	bells	5904	hogs
3704918	big hole	3704	hole
55378	bless	771	ill
55178	bliss	73817	libel
57108	boils	5907	logs
5008	boos	717	li'l (little)
32008	booze	5317717	lillies
5508	boss	217	liz
37818	Bible	3807	lobe
5379908	boggles	5107	lois
8008	boob	3790	ogle
993	egg	710	oil
173	eli	335	see
35339	geese	32135	seize
5379919	giggles	39135	seige
57719	gills	7735	sell
3379	glee	5808345	she bobs
38079	globe	5317345	she lies
0.9	go	5805345	she sobs
5309	goes	407145	shiloh
53551434	he hisses	4915	sigh
9185134	he is big	515	sis
81795134	he is glib	372215	sizzle
5350734	he loses	58075	slobs
7734	hell	45075	slosh
23534	he sez	705	sol
4914	high	l3705	sole
7714	hill	7105	soil
3379514	his glee	0.02	zoo
53045514	his shoes		

Contributors

ORDER FORM

Mail to: SCHUMACHER ENTERPRISES
2629 Manhattan Ave., PMB 215
Hermosa Beach, CA 90254-2447
E-mail: mschuma233@aol.com
Fax 1-949-916-5219

I wish to purchase_____copies of

The Spirit of

DAVID

(Proceeds to Charity)

Total price is $19.00 per copy out of state,

includes postage & handling.

California residents are 20.00 per copy

Price includes book at $14.95 per copy plus tax $1.24

plus postage & handling of $3.81

Enclosed please find payment of $_____
❑ Check (Payable to Schumacher Enterprises)
❑ Money Order or Credit Card: ❑ Visa ❑ Mastercard
Credit card number _____
Name on card (print LEGIBLY) _____
Signature of cardholder _____

Send order to: (PLEASE PRINT LEGIBLY)
Name_____
Address_____Apt. #_____
City_____State_____Zip_____
Phone ( ) _____
DISCOUNTS FOR MULTIPLE BOOK ORDERS
Individuals or groups, fundraising for charity, etc., please email
mschuma233@aol.com for more information